GUIDING BLIGHT

GOOD TO THE LAST DEMON

BOOK 4

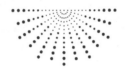

ROBYN PETERMAN

JOIN MY NEWSLETTER!

ACKNOWLEDGMENTS

The Guiding Blight is book 4 in a spinoff of The Good To The Last Death Series. You don't have to have read the other series, but there are fun shout outs for those who have. Candy Vargo makes a big appearance in this one.

I wrote The Facts of Midlife knowing I was going to spin Abaddon off into his own series.
And then I came up with the perfect heroine.

I promised myself a very long time ago that someday I would write a story about an actress and use some of my real life experiences…
That time has come. LOL
The names have been changed to protect the innocent and the guilty.

The situations have been slightly altered.
Clearly, I'm not a Demon—well not on a daily basis.
Cecily, our new and fabulous heroine, is a Demon.

So get ready for a wild, wild ride. I had a blast writing The Bold and the Banished and hope you love reading about Abaddon and Cecily.

As always, writing may be a solitary sport, but it takes a bunch of terrific people to get a book out into the world.

Renee — Thank you for my beautiful cover and for being the best badass critique partner in the world. TMB. LOL

Wanda — You are the freaking bomb. Love you to the moon and back.

Heather, Nancy, Susan, Caroline and Wanda — Thank you for reading early and helping me find the booboos. You all saved my ass. You rock.

My Readers — Thank you for loving the stories that come from my warped mind. It thrills me.

Steve, Henry and Audrey — Your love and support makes all of this so much more fun. I love you people endlessly.

DEDICATION

For my Cookie. You saved my butt. I owe you a box!

MORE IN THE GOOD TO THE LAST DEMON SERIES

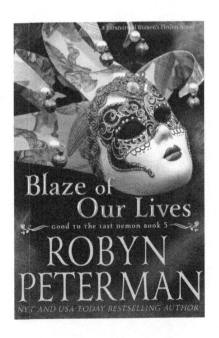

ORDER BOOK 5 NOW!

BOOK DESCRIPTION

GUIDING BLIGHT

I crashed the Immortal party and it ended with a surprise encore... a big one.

I thought being a Demon sucked, but being a Demon Goddess is a whole 'nother level. Life had been so much easier when I was just a forty-year-old has-been actress trying to make a comeback in the land of Botox and BS.

For the love of everything absurd, I was just getting used to being a Demon... and BAM... all of a sudden I'm supposed to be one of the two gals in charge? I mean, being the co-star of the show is great until it involves ruling the Darkness with the evil whack job who destroyed my mother.

Pandora is a guiding blight in my world, and I plan to cancel her at all costs. With my Demon love by my side and a gaggle os Immortal nutbags along for the ride, I'll find the vicious Goddess and put her back in her box.

Ah well, fate is set. Destiny is my performance to command. I plan it improv the heck out of it. Go big or go home is my new modus operandi. Although, right now, home sounds seriously appealing. Either way, I'm strapping in and getting ready for the wildest gig yet.

CHAPTER ONE

ON THE OTHER SIDE OF THE DOOR WAS MY FATHER.

On the other side of the door was my mortal enemy, who'd kidnapped my dad.

Opening the door could end me. Not opening could end him.

I had a choice, and I'd already made my decision. Opening the door was a no-brainer.

But first, I had to protect the people who had fought to protect me.

My life had been a hell of a lot easier when I was just an over-the-hill actress in her forties, trying to make a comeback.

I took a hesitant step toward the door, assessing my options.

"Wait," Stella hissed, getting to her feet. The Demon might've been a crappy actress with entirely too much Botox and giant knockers that doubled as weapons, but in the short time we'd been together, she had become one of my most trusted nearest and dearest.

"What's going on?" I asked.

She brushed herself off, then closed her eyes for a moment and wiggled her hips. "I sense six flaming assholes in there, not counting the shitty whore, Pandora, and your father."

"Is Pandora stupid?" I asked my small posse telepathically. Since they'd pledged their loyalty to me as their new Demon goddess—a title I'd very reluctantly accepted, I could talk with them in their minds. It was incredibly handy. As to the matter at hand... Pandora had obviously watched the smackdown we'd had with her assassins a short and bloody time ago. A smart Demon would have reinforced the troops. Not to mention, she knew we were right outside of her door. The whirring of the cameras was loud.

"That's a given," Jonny, who was turning out not to be an idiot, whispered. "Her power and ego know no bounds. Las Vegas and the greater state of Nevada are her territories. She feels almighty here."

"Aesop," Moon Sunny Swartz said.

It was an odd non sequitur. I glanced over at her in confusion. Moon was an excellent weapon of mass confusion.

"He was a Greek storyteller," she explained.

"I know that," I said. *"Is there a reason you brought him up?"*

"Fabulous guy," Corny, who was thankfully no longer naked, commented with a nod. Granted he could fly easier while in the buff, but seeing his wrinkled junk had been gag inducing. "Great drinking buddy."

I was reminded again of how long the company I was keeping had lived. I pushed the hard-to-imagine concept away and focused on Moon. *"What about Aesop?"*

"He said, the smaller the mind, the greater the conceit."

Irma, no longer in her shifted mouse form, added her two cents. "He also stated, conceit may bring about one's own downfall."

"Sage words," Stella approved, patting both Irma and Moon on their backs. "I'd like to take a vote."

What the heck was happening here? We had a mission to accomplish. *"Vote?"* I asked in a stressed tone.

"Yes," she said. "I vote that we call our movie, *Aesop's Badass Demons Kick the Shitty Whore's Ass.*"

It was kind of useless at this point to remind them this wasn't a movie. It was unscripted reality. But they were actors, albeit fairly talent-free. If pretending this was a movie helped them cope with the dangerous situation, I was all for it.

I winced. *"Umm... that's a really long title."*

"How about *Aesop's Assholes?"* Jonny suggested. "The alliteration is nice, and the bitch Goddess Cecily is pulling the plot out of her ass."

"Oscar-worthy," Corny announced. "I love it."

I blew out a frustrated raspberry. *"Fine. Aesop's Assholes for the win. Happy?"*

"Very," Irma said. "Way better to star in *Aesop's Assholes* than be the spokeswoman for vaginal itch cream." She gave Moon the stink eye and a middle finger salute.

Moon returned the rude gesture with a grin.

I laughed. I couldn't help it. These whackadoos had lessened my stress. I wasn't sure if that was their intention or a by-product of their weirdness. Didn't matter. The result was welcome.

"Aesop did so love to get gussied up," Corny said.

My never-ending curiosity perked up. Plus, Candy Vargo had said there were no stupid questions. That was up for debate, but whatever. *"Gussied up?"*

"Loved a little makeup," Corny explained with a giggle. "Especially lip rouge. He wore it well!"

A zing of energy shot through me at his admission. Candy Vargo for the win. There were *no* stupid questions. And also, a big shout out to Shiva for the makeup weapons. Becoming her semi-hostile BFF was on the to-do list.

"Do you have your lipsticks?" I asked, checking my pocket for mine. It was there.

My Demons nodded.

"Six flaming assholes. Six lipsticks. On my command, we use them on her flunkies. It'll give us a better chance at survival."

"That's suspect," Stella said. "I detect a hole in the plot."

"Tell me," I said. We were working as a team. While they might be questionable actors, I wasn't a full-time writer.

"If we attack them with the *ipsticklay*, it will look like we are on *uoryay idesay*. The shitty whore will not believe our *oyaltylay* is to *erhay*."

I couldn't believe I followed that, but I did. And she was correct. The lipstick maneuver was a dead giveaway that we were working together. Part of the plan was for them to pretend they were still loyal to their old Goddess, Pandora. Screwing that up could put my dad in even more danger.

I racked my brain and came up with a rewrite on the

scene. Pulling it out of my ass was an understatement. *"Okay... Moon, you hum quietly on my command. That will make them come at us without provocation. Make it look like self-defense then throw yourselves on Pandora's mercy. Get close to my dad and get him out of here."*

"Genius," Corny congratulated me. "Am I still the one chosen to transport your father?"

I paused for a moment. *"Yes,"* I told him, but I left out a big plot twist. When Corny had my dad, they were all leaving. This was my fight, and they weren't going to die for me.

They were not going to be happy, but I was the Goddess, writer, leading actor, and director *of Aesop's Assholes.* I was looking at the big picture, and my word was law.

"Are we ready?" I asked.

"Hell to the yes," Moon answered.

I went straight to my new catch phrase. It applied perfectly. *"Let's get this party started."*

And we did.

I'D SEEN THE IMAGE OF PANDORA AND MAN-MOM ON THE monitors only minutes earlier, but nothing could have prepared me for the real thing. My dad's labored breathing and ashen skin triggered a fury that bubbled up inside me. I wanted to rip the Demon Goddess limb from limb. Rational thought was almost impossible. I made eye contact with dad, and he weakly shook his head. He wanted me to leave. That wasn't happening.

"You're a fucking bitch," Irma snarled at me, punctuating it with an electrical volt.

Pandora laughed. It was slimy and made my skin crawl. However, I was wildly grateful to Irma Stoutwagon. She sensed my distress and zapped me out of it. Literally. Her acting chops were better than I'd originally thought.

"Screw you," I hissed back at her. "It's time for me to end all of you so I win the prize."

The flaming assholes guarding Pandora bared their teeth. I was pretty sure they were smiling at the antics, but it was terrifying.

"I'm winning," Moon shouted, throwing daggers like confetti. "All of your pathetic asses are grass."

"In your dreams," Stella growled, punching Moon in the head and sending her flying.

The shitty whore clasped her hands in delight. A blood-bath was clearly her idea of a good time. Her lackeys enjoyed the show as well. Violence was held in high regard.

It was time to get the audience involved.

"Moon, hum," I directed as I dropped kicked Corny into Jonny.

The tune was barely audible over the shouts and vicious insults from me and my people, but it did the trick. The flaming assholes' gazes went blank, and they began to advance. Moon's talent was impossible for them to escape.

"Stop!" Pandora commanded. "I want them to end each other. Better for ratings."

They didn't listen. The pull of Moon's magical song was too much.

The battle grew vicious. I'd taken a claw to the face but

had kicked the flaming asshole's balls up into his esophagus. It only stopped him for thirty seconds. He came at me like a nuclear weapon. All of my people were bleeding, and a few body parts had been ripped off. I wasn't sure who was missing appendages. There was no time to assess the situation without getting decapitated. That scene wasn't in this movie.

We'd battled long enough to make it look real.

"Lipsticks. NOW," I shouted in their minds.

On cue, Corny, Jonny, Stella, Irma, Moon and I tased the flaming assholes. They went down with loud thuds. Pandora's confusion at the turn of events set her off. She glowed a blinding silver and grabbed my father by the neck.

"What is happening?" she bellowed as she began to choke the life out of Bill Bloom.

"Beg for mercy. NOW," I directed.

I reassessed my idea that they were bad actors. My ragtag crew gave Oscar-worthy performances.

"Oh, beautiful Goddess Pandora," Irma cried out, throwing herself at Pandora's feet. She was missing a leg and an arm. "I beg of you to take me back. I worship you. I have lived in agony and devastation without you."

"You killed my most trusted generals," she hissed, electrocuting Irma.

"No," Irma screamed, writhing on the ground in pain. "They're not dead, just incapacitated. I swear. It was self-defense. You saw it."

Pandora considered Irma's words as she squeezed harder on my father's neck. It took effort I didn't know I possessed to not stop the scene and end her. Abaddon had told me I wasn't capable of ending her. I knew with all my heart he was wrong.

"My Goddess Pandora," Corny said in a trembling voice I'd never heard him use. "I am your humble servant. I don't care about winning the prize. I just want to win back your trust."

He crawled on all fours to her feet. She kicked him in the head with her stiletto-clad heels, but he crawled back for more.

Jonny, Moon and Stella followed their fellow actors' leads and begged for forgiveness. The shitty whore bought it hook, line and sinker.

I stood across the room, separated from my people. I schooled my face in an expression of disdain for the weak Demons who pled for her acceptance at her feet.

Pandora's gaze met mine. Her eyes narrowed to slits... then she smiled. "Guess you lose, Cecily Bloom. The prize goes to my people." She waved her hand. "What say you, we turn off the cameras and let the end play out a mystery?"

The whir of the cameras ceased. My stomach cramped. Abaddon, Lilith and Dagon could no longer see the feed. The Demon I loved, my mother, and the other Demon I considered a friend were in the dark. If they came too early, Man-mom would die. If they came too late, I would.

I was about to be on my own.

The heinous Goddess tossed my father to the Demons groveling at her feet. She was so focused on me that she didn't see their grins of delight. Once I spotted Man-mom wrapped in Corny's embrace, I gave the final direction to the actors in *Aesop's Assholes*. The movie would continue, but their roles were being retired. I didn't know how the film would end, but I knew how the current scene was about to play out.

"*Plot twist,*" I said in a brook-no-bullshit tone. "*All of you are leaving now. Pandora wants me, not you. You're my people, and I won't let you die.*"

My little army's looks of shock and distress were real.

"*No, negotiating,*" I said sternly. "*The minute Corny leaves with my dad, the jig is up. You will obey me. I'm the director and your Goddess. If I bite it, tell Abaddon I love him. Send Candy Vargo a thank you note for the toothpicks and for believing that I was a badass from the get-go. Tell my dad, my brother and dead Uncle Joe that I'll try to come back as a ghost. Tell my agent Cher that I want her to represent all of you. Let Fifi and Ophelia know that they can have my house and get Fifi some earplugs to block out Ophelia's snoring. I'm proud to call you my friends. You're truly amazing Demons. It's an honor to be your Goddess. And most importantly, hug Lilith and tell her it's from me. She'll understand.*"

Moon had tears running down her face. Even with the Botox, I could see Stella was devastated. Corny held my dad close and nodded in respect to me.

Irma couldn't contain herself. "That's a fuck ton to remember, bitch," she shrieked. "I'm not good at memorization."

"I'm an excellent thespian," Jonny yelled. "I have taken mental note of everything. It shall be done."

"What are you babbling about?" Pandora demanded, electrocuting them. "You will speak when you're spoken to or it will end badly... for you. Kill the human," she insisted, staring daggers at the Demons surrounding her. "Prove your loyalty to me. It will be icing on the cake for Cecily Bloom to watch her father die."

"*Leave. Immediately,*" I commanded them.

In a puff of red shimmering mist, they disappeared with my father cradled safely in Corny's arms.

Pandora's expression of utter shock would have been funny in another time and on another planet. "Well, aren't you the clever one, Cecily Bloom," she purred with venom dripping off of each over-enunciated word. "I didn't realize you were that deviously smart."

For a hot sec, I considered taking a hard left in the plot and weaving in a shitty movie I'd done called *You're Not My Mother*. It had come to mind when I was at Candy Vargo's big white mansion. Had that been a sign? In the crappy B movie, I'd successfully convinced the nightmare of a woman who'd kidnapped me that I was on her side. I'd kept her going until the police arrived.

Pandora wasn't that stupid. She'd never believe I'd defect to her side no matter how good of an actress I was. However, most narcissists loved to talk about themselves. If I could get her talking, I'd buy some time.

"How did you get out of the time-out?" I questioned.

Her brow raised. She refused to speak.

Compliment the ego… "Impressive. Candy Vargo isn't someone who makes many mistakes. Your power must eclipse hers."

I didn't believe that for a second, but Pandora took the bait. She was thrilled.

"No one can trap me," she snarled. "I am the Goddess Pandora. I'm more powerful than all."

"Seems that way," I said, snapping my fingers and producing a chair. I sat down and crossed my legs.

She was taken aback at my casual demeanor.

"What do you think you're doing?" she hissed.

I shrugged and smiled. More likely than not, I was about to die. She knew it and I knew it. I'd give her a run for her money, but she was a gazillion years old and I was forty. The odds were not in my favor. "Well, since I'm about to bite it, I figured I'd get a few questions answered first. You have a problem with that?"

She wavered for a moment. With a wiggle of her fingers, she repaired her throne and sat down. "Your bravery is surprising."

"That's a compliment coming from you," I told her flatly.

She wasn't sure if I was being serious or sarcastic. I didn't help her out. "How did you learn of my existence?"

"Wouldn't you like to know," she sneered.

"Actually, yes. That's why I asked."

She was thrown easily. I wasn't kissing her ass. I wasn't afraid of her either. She didn't know what to do with the situation at hand. I felt a sudden sense of peace. I wouldn't die as a coward. I wouldn't beg for my life. That would bring her too much pleasure.

Whatever. It was just her and me now. I crossed my fingers and sent good vibes out into the Universe that backup was about to arrive. Man-mom was safe. Even though I might not survive, it was time for all of Hell to rain down on Pandora.

"Do you not recall who told you about me?" I queried.

"Of course, I do," she snapped. "She's dead."

My brows shot up. I knew it had been Rhoda Spark—the Demon who had kidnapped Abaddon when he had been weak and then handed him over to Pandora. She had pretended to be loyal to Lilith, much the same way I'd had my Demon army pretend. She'd been on Team Pandora all along. Unfortunately, the reward for her blind faith in evil had been the reason for her demise. She'd annoyed Pandora and died violently at her hand because of it.

"Rhoda Spark," I said aloud.

"Correct." Pandora cracked her neck, stretched her arms, and finished with a yawn. "I'm getting bored and itching to murder you. You can have one last question."

"And you'll answer it?" I challenged.

She rolled her eyes and waited.

No question was stupid... "Is Pandora's box a real thing?"

For only the briefest second the vile woman's eyes went wide with fear. It was so fleeting, it could have been easily missed. I didn't miss things like that. Human nature fascinated me. From an early age, I'd studied people. I'd always thought I did it because I was an actress. Now, I wondered if fate had something else in store for me with that particular talent.

"Answer the question, Pandora."

She eyed me like I was an insect she was about to swat. "The box exists. However, you're going to take that secret to the grave, Cecily Bloom." She stood up and tossed her waist-length raven-black hair over her shoulder. "I was going to kill you slowly, but you pulled one over on me with those deplorable Demons. For that, I shall reward you with a quick demise."

A knot formed in my throat. I didn't take her threat lightly. I didn't have any doubt that she had the power to end my life. It was devastating to think that I would never see Man-mom, Uncle Joe and Sean again, but I knew they'd be fine. My death would ensure their safety.

When I pictured Abaddon's handsome face, my heart broke. I loved him and he loved me. The only solace I had was that we'd cleared up the miscommunication. He'd be okay too. He had to be.

And Lilith… it ate at me that I hadn't hugged my mother. I'd wanted to but held back. It was a good lesson in not leaving things undone. It was too late now. In another moment of clarity, I realized I would have done the same as she'd done if the roles were reversed and she was my daughter. She loved me enough to let me live. Leaving me was a selfless act. I hoped to Hell and back that when I died, I could come back as a ghost like Uncle Joe. Telling her I loved her would be one of the first things I did.

"Am I supposed to thank you for that?"

She hissed and growled like an animal. Apparently, it was okay for her to be a nasty bitch, but she didn't like it when the favor was returned.

Too bad, so sad.

The air in the room grew frigid and a sickly-sweet scented wind whipped through. Pandora clapped her hands and produced her purple fire sword. I smiled. I wasn't going down without a fight. I held my hands out and produced two.

She was not pleased.

"Get ready to die, Cecily Bloom," she bellowed.

The building shook with her rage. I stood my ground and waited for her to come at me. Dagon had said there was strength in stillness. I was going to take his advice.

The building continued to tremble. Chunks of the ceiling fell to the floor, and the silver throne Pandora had sat upon erupted into flame.

"Stop it," she ground out. "I will not be so kind with your death if you defy me."

I wasn't doing it, but that was for me to know and for her to never find out.

When the lighting fixtures exploded, all of my wishes came true. Lilith, Abaddon and Dagon appeared in a hail of black glitter and silver mist. Pandora's fury at the twist in the scene was only eclipsed by my mother's.

"You're cheating," Pandora screamed at me with spittle coming out of her mouth.

"That's rich coming from you, shitty whore," I shot back.

The vicious Goddess waved her hand. In a flash of lightning and a crash of thunder, at least fifty flaming assholes appeared. The smile on her lips was psychotic. "Kill Cecily Bloom!"

Lilith, Dagon, Abaddon and I fought the army of evil with all we had… and we had a lot. My mother was a freaking killing machine. She was balletic, precise and terrifying. For the most part, the flaming assholes avoided her. They knew who she was and that ending her was forbidden.

Dagon was no slouch, but Abaddon fought like a crazed animal.

Blow by blow. Electrocution by electrocution. It was a bloody mess. I'd lost part of my left hand but was still able to grip my sword.

Pandora stood back and watched. Her cowardice was astounding. I might die, but she was going down.

The enemy went from fifty down to twelve quickly. However, the last dozen were determined.

"Cecily, leave," Lilith yelled over the ruckus. "Now."

I wanted to obey her. I really did, but I couldn't. This was my battle. I needed to fight it. "Not until she's back in her box," I shouted.

Everything that came next happened fast, but I would replay it in slow motion for the rest of my days. Pandora began to lob explosive fireballs. I screamed in agony when one hit my leg. I refused to look down to see if my leg was still there. The searing pain nauseated me. Moving away from the sizzling fire, I realized that even though I had third-degree burns, or worse, I could still walk. Which meant, both legs were still intact.

I kept my eyes on Pandora's hands while trying to defend myself from her Demons.

Abaddon was at my side immediately. In the millisecond it took for me to acknowledge him, I saw a flaming asshole come up behind him wielding a fiery sword.

"Duck," I shouted at the love of my life.

Abaddon escaped the beheading, but Pandora took my distraction as her opening. The ball of fire she hurled at me was massive, deadly and had my name all over it. I tried to dodge it, but my leg hindered my escape. The aggressive push from my right side sent me flying into Abaddon. The explosion was brutal. The building creaked on its foundation.

Dagon's furious roar made me lightheaded. "What have you done?"

"It's not my fault," Pandora shrieked at the accusing Demon. I could swear she was having a panic attack. The evil Goddess pulled on her hair and ran her sharp nails down her arms leaving behind trails of oozing blood.

I couldn't understand what was happening... until I did.

Lilith had collapsed on the floor where I had been only seconds ago. Her beautiful body was broken and battered. She bled profusely from her mouth and her chest wasn't moving. The light was gone. Her life was gone.

The realization was hard to comprehend. It didn't make any sense, but the proof was in front of me. She'd died for me. My mother had brought me into this world, and now she'd sacrificed herself to keep me in it. This was all wrong. I'd never told my mother I loved her. I'd never hugged her. Now I'd never get the chance.

I'd heard about seeing red but hadn't experienced it until now. My body heated up like a roaring furnace. My tongue felt like steaming hot sandpaper and my vision blurred with hatred. With a scream of rage so raw I was sure my throat would bleed, I slashed my hands through the air. The last twelve flaming assholes combusted into flames while screaming in agony. The six who had been stunned by the lipsticks exploded as well. Good riddance to horrible rubbish.

My lips stretched thin and wide into a wretched smile that didn't reach my eyes. "Eighteen down," I hissed at Pandora. "One to go. Get ready to die."

I ran at her with inhuman speed in a fit of all-consuming anger. My purple fire swords were aimed at her neck. She would pay, and I would exact the payment.

As I swung my swords with all my might, Pandora disappeared in a blast of black glitter. I fell to the ground from the intensity of my blows that hadn't even touched her. I stared in shock at the ground where she'd stood only moments before.

"No, no, no," I cried out.

Abaddon's arms around me from behind felt safe and loving. I pushed him away. I didn't want, nor did I deserve, safe and loving. My mother had died because of me.

I stood and approached her body slowly. I wanted to peel off my skin to cover my grief with physical pain. I fought back the tears, afraid that if they started, I would cry forever. Dagon wept as he stood guard over his Goddess's body. Abaddon wept as well.

I was so distraught the tears wouldn't come.

Getting down on my knees, I wrapped my arms around my mother the way I should have yesterday and the day before. I hugged her lifeless body close and breathed in her scent. Forever be damned, I thought, as flood gates opened. The tears came naturally as my mind raced with all the things I'd miss without her here.

"I was supposed to teach you how to drive," I whispered brokenly. "You're a terrible driver."

I tried to wipe the blood from her face but smeared it instead.

Abaddon gently touched my back.

This time I didn't pull away. "I never told her I loved her," I choked out, still desperately trying to clean her up with the sleeve of my shirt. "She told me she loved me, and I didn't say anything."

"She knew," Abaddon said softly.

I shook my head. "But I didn't tell her. I'll never get to tell her. I called her Lilith, not Mom."

Sobs racked my body as I held on to the woman who had traded her life for mine. My guilt overwhelmed me, and I wished I could go back in time. It wasn't possible. Some things weren't possible no matter how much you believed or wished on stars.

"We can't stay here," Dagon finally said in a hushed and brokenhearted tone. "It's not safe, Goddess Cecily. We must return Lilith's body to the Darkness before she turns to dust."

I glanced over at him. He got down on his knees and bowed to me. Abaddon did the same.

"No," I said quickly. "No. Don't."

Abaddon raised his head and stood back up. His gaze was intense. It made me feel out of control and breathless.

"You're her heir, Cecily," he said. "It's fated."

I pressed my lips together so I wouldn't scream. I wasn't the Goddess of the Darkness. I was Cecily Bloom, a former child star who was about to make a comeback in a new TV series. Dagon and Abaddon had lost their damned minds if they thought I could be the Goddess of the Darkness and replace my mother.

"It's what your mother would want," Dagon said, standing up as well.

I glanced over at him like he was nuts. "She'd want a forty-year-old actress who just found out she was a Demon to run the show? Lilith might have been a shitty driver, but she wasn't insane. I'm not fit to fill her shoes."

Dagon smiled at me. It was a sad smile, but it was real. "I promise you this is what she would want. You're her daughter—her blood. You're a born Goddess. I'll be at your side every step of the way."

"As will I," Abaddon added. "I believe in you, Cecily."

I leaned in and gently kissed my mother's forehead. "I'm not sure I believe in me."

Abaddon squatted down next to me. "How about I believe in you enough for both of us?"

I gave him a weak smile and nodded.

Fate was set. Destiny was mine to mold. Shit. Life had just taken a U-turn into Hell. Literally.

Lilith's body began to glow and shimmer. Dagon gasped. Abaddon was speechless and open-mouthed.

"What's wrong?" I asked, as the delicate magic swirled around my mother and me.

Dagon shook his head. He was frantic. "I don't know what's happening."

I held my mother closer, trying to keep her from disappearing. The enchantment continued to dance around us as Lilith's broken body began to fade away. In a pop of iridescent silver mist, she was gone.

I was frozen to the spot.

"What the Hell?" Abaddon questioned in a perplexed and alarmed tone.

"I truly don't know," Dagon said as he began pacing erratically. "She should have turned to dust. Even then, it shouldn't have been this fast. There should've been time for me to return her body to the Darkness."

My hackles rose. "Is it Pandora? Did she steal my mother's body?"

Abaddon growled.

Dagon held up a hand. "I don't believe Pandora had anything to do with this. It was far too peaceful."

Glancing down at where my mother used to be, I felt the tears come on again. I was going to be crying for a while. "What do we do?" I asked, sniffling.

"We get out of here," Abaddon said. "We're in Pandora's territory."

"And what about her? She's supposed to be in time-out," I reminded the men.

"The Grim Reaper and the Keeper of Fate are on it," Dagon informed me. "We shall aid them as necessary."

"Her box is real," I told them.

Both men's brows shot up.

"Do you know where it is?" Abaddon asked.

"No," I told him. "But you'd better believe I'm going to find it."

"I've already told you I believe in you," he said. "I have no doubt you'll find Pandora's box. And I'll be at your side when you do."

I nodded. Exhaustion made me feel dizzy. There was

nothing left here that I cared about except Abaddon and Dagon. "It's time to go. I need to see Man-mom."

"As you wish, Goddess Cecily," Dagon said with another bow of respect.

The bowing was going to take some getting used to. Honestly, I liked the title 'Bitch Goddess Cecily' better, but would save that for another conversation. I didn't see it going over well.

Abaddon's cell phone rang. I was surprised it worked, but the shitty whore was gone. Her spells must have left with her.

He glanced down at it and tilted his head in surprise. "It's your father," he said, handing me his phone.

My stomach flipped. I couldn't take any more bad news. Quickly, I answered. "Man-mom?"

"Cecily-boo," he said. "I was so worried."

He sounded tired and happy, but his voice was hoarse as if he'd been crying.

"I'm fine," I lied. I wasn't sure I was going to be fine ever again. "Are you okay?"

"I am," he said, sounding strange. Not scared strange... just really strange.

"Mmkay," I said. "I'm coming home now."

"That's good, Cecily-boo. I love you," he said. "There's someone here who wants to see you."

"I love you too. Tell Sean and Uncle Joe I'm on my way," I said with a smile.

I knew I'd have to tell Man-mom about Lilith. He'd be heartbroken. I'd take him to the safehouse, so he could see how much she'd always loved him... and me.

"Not Sean and Joe," he said with a silly lightness in his voice that I'd never heard.

"Should I guess?" I asked, catching his silliness.

"I don't think you'll be able to," he replied with a chuckle.

"Okay, I give up. Who's waiting to see me?"

He took a deep breath and blew it out slowly. The suspense was killing me. "Your mother. Your mother is home, and this time, she's here to stay."

I couldn't say a word. Dropping the phone, I started to sob. Abaddon's phone shattered into pieces. Sean and I had been worried about our dad's memory for a while. His bout with Pandora had clearly sent him over the edge. I pivoted my gaze to Abaddon and mouthed, "He thinks my mother is with him."

Abaddon squinted at me then glanced over at Dagon. "Is that possible?" he asked.

"No. I don't think so," Dagon replied.

"Is it Pandora?" Abaddon ground out.

"She's in hiding," Dagon surmised. "More importantly, Bill didn't seem to be in danger. Shiva, Cher, Fifi and Ophelia are there along with Corny, Irma, Stella, Moon and Jonny. The street is also warded. There's no way for Pandora to have entered Cecily's home."

Abaddon put his hand under my chin and gently raised my tear-stained gaze to his. "I'm not sure who is with your father, but we need to find out. Are you up to it?"

I wiped my tears and lightly kissed his lips. "No. But that's never stopped me yet."

"Take my hands," Dagon urged, clearly unnerved. "We must go at once."

I had no clue who my dad thought was my mother, but whoever was messing with him and us would be very sorry shortly.

In a blast of chilly wind and glittering black mist, we headed to the next adventure.

And what an adventure it would turn out to be...

CHAPTER TWO

WE MATERIALIZED IN A GUST OF SILVER AND BLACK shimmering magic on the street directly in front of my house. Abaddon stood on my right and Dagon on my left. The tension was palpable. On either side of the walkway leading to the front door were Demons, Succubi and a single Angel.

I feared none of them. They were my friends.

I was aware of their presence, but my eyes were drawn to the front porch. My breath caught in my throat, and a tingle of dread outweighed by delight came close to making my knees buckle. Abaddon sensed my distress and lent me a strong arm to stay steady. The man was not only hot but handy as well. I was unsure if he and Dagon were as shocked as I was, but a gentle breeze could have blown me over. The vision didn't make sense, but nothing in my life made all that much sense anymore.

"Breathe," Abaddon said softly.

"Trying," I muttered, still staring at the unbelievable gathering on my porch.

The sun could have exploded and I wouldn't have noticed. The picture in front of me was one I'd longed for my entire life. It was much different than the image I'd imagined as a child, but no less gorgeous.

I'd pictured myself as a little girl, standing between them. Protected by them. Loved by them. That was then. This was now. I was loved, but I was basically on my own for protection. The thought was too much to handle without losing my mind. Pushing the stark reality away, I focused on the scene in front of me.

It felt like a surreal movie.

It wasn't. There was no question in my mind if it was actually her. I knew the woman at a bone-deep level even though I'd barely spent any time with her. I couldn't help but feel it had all come too late. That was incredibly selfish. I knew it, but letting the thought go wasn't easy. Analyzing was a waste of time I wasn't sure I had. Forcing myself to stay in the moment, I tried to memorize what I was seeing. The thought that it could disappear in an instant terrified me.

Man-mom's smile was so wide it almost made my cheeks hurt for him. To his right stood my brother, Sean. My nutty—and probably high—sibling's smile was a bit perplexed but was as wide as our father's. Dead Uncle Joe, in all his ghostly, naked and wrinkled glory, floated in the air above Sean, giggling like a fool. His hands were clasped tightly and he quivered with excitement. Unfortunately, his *entire* body quivered. While it was alarming to notice my beloved relative's junk jiggling, I was able to ignore it. While bouncing ghost bits were kind of difficult to disregard, I did it. I was successful because there was something stunningly beautiful to look at.

On Man-mom's left stood the woman. The very same woman who I'd held dead in my arms only moments ago. She looked very different. She was no longer covered in smeared blood. She was no longer lifeless. She didn't look forty years old anymore. The woman was no less ravishing. Lilith appeared to be around sixty-five years old—the same age as my dad. The lines around her eyes when she smiled brought tears to mine.

Tears of complete joy.

"Mom?" I whispered through a choked sob. Something held me back from running to her. Possibly fear that I was imagining everything and if I took a step forward reality would rear its ugly head.

She nodded and winked. "I've come home, Cecily," she answered. "This time I'm here to stay."

Squinting my eyes, I gasped.

Lilith was no longer a Demon—or at least not *all* Demon. She appeared mostly human with the slightest Immortal glow around her that was quickly fading. Again, the truth smacked me like a ton of cinder blocks. Lilith was not the Demon Goddess of the Darkness anymore...

I was.

Shit.

Or... maybe not.

"How?" I asked as I slowly approached, still scared that she would disappear.

Lilith shrugged and shook her head. Her amazement was as obvious as mine.

Ophelia stepped forward. She bowed to me then to Lilith. "As the legend goes, if a Goddess loses her Immortality, she becomes human."

Corny Crackers joined Ophelia. "Yes, yes! Granted, it's not happened until now, but the Tome of Dark Magic prophesized it millions of years ago. Lilith is now a human! And Cecily is the new Goddess of the Darkness along with the shitty whore, Pandora. All hail the Bitch Goddess Cecily!" Corny Crackers shouted as he dropped to his knees in front of me.

Ophelia and her double D rack that she'd paid good money for spun around and punched Corny in the head. "What the actual F did you just call her?"

Fifi, my six feet tall self-proclaimed Succubus bodyguard, pulled grenades from her pockets and aimed them at Corny. She was gorgeous, intimidating and had a resting bitch face like none I'd ever witnessed. My bodyguard also offered to bang my enemies to death on the regular. That was never going to happen. And watching Corny get his head blown off by a grenade wasn't going to happen either.

To make matters more dangerous, Stella had removed her shirt and was boobs to the wind. Normally, that would just be considered really bad manners to disrobe in public. Crappy manners aside, Stella's knockers were weapons. They shot bullets. Irma Stoutwagon looked ready for a smackdown, and Moon Sunny Swartz was doing pushups. Jonny had gone invisible. The scent of rotten eggs was the giveaway. I had no clue where he was and that was not a good thing.

Sushi, the ten-thousand-year-old Succubi Queen and award-winning costumer to the stars, wasn't pleased with the scene playing out and exposed her five inch pointed fangs that I was unaware she possessed.

Abaddon began to glow and growl. Dagon had pulled a vicious looking sword. And my agent, Cher was lining her lips with a green eye pencil like her life depended on it.

Shit had gone south.

"Nope, nope, nope," I yelled, getting between Fifi and the end of Corny while pulling on my newly found magic and producing two purple fire swords. Thankfully, the flaming blades made them pause. "Everyone, stand down or you're going to lose a body part. I am not f-ing around."

Ophelia tossed her blonde curls and threw her hands in the air. "But that prolapsed anus just called you a bitch."

I rolled my eyes and shook my head. "You call me a bitch all the time," I reminded her.

"Yesssss," she hissed. "That's my loving fucking nick-name for you."

I transferred the fire sword in my left hand over to my right so I had a free hand to press the bridge of my nose. I was dealing with idiots. Most of them were actors or wannabe actors. I'd treat this like a show... or a shitshow to be more accurate.

"Here's the deal," I announced. "I like the title Bitch Goddess Cecily. It's so wrong, it's right. Like any good stage name, it's unforgettable."

Ophelia looked confused. Not surprising. Corny, Stella,

Moon, Irma and a partially corporeal Jonny nodded in agreement. Cher printed out the name on the sidewalk with her green eye pencil. After examining it for a moment, she gave me a thumbs up. Fifi put the grenades back into her pockets and Sushi's terrifying fangs retracted. Everyone was out of their damned minds—me included. I stole a quick glance at my mother. She was doing her best not to laugh. While I didn't disagree that the situation was somewhat humorous, I'd already dealt with a bunch of bloodshed today on top of a death and a resurrection.

I was over it. "Also, it's debatable if the stage name will be necessary." I crossed my fingers and took a deep breath. Ripping off the band-aid was my new modus operandi. Guessing wasn't good for my sanity or my digestive system. "Lilith is still alive. So… umm… I'm hoping that she can still do the job of Goddess and I'm off the hook or the show… so to speak."

My friends and family were still confused.

I clarified, "You know, like I was hired then fired."

Still mass confusion. I'd clearly been hanging out with Moon Sunny Swartz and Ophelia too often.

"Look at it this way…" I gestured to my mother. "Lilith is the star of the show. On opening night, she gets food poisoning."

Corny raised his hand. I nodded at him.

"Bad food poisoning?" he asked. "Like puking and blowing it out of your ass food poisoning?"

I quickly retracted my purple fire swords so I didn't lop his head off. "Umm… sure," I replied. "Anyhoo, I'm her seriously underprepared and freaked-out understudy. BUT, right before places are called, Lilith makes a miraculous recovery and goes on. Which is fabulous, considering I don't know any of my lines or blocking, and I don't have any costumes."

"So, you were prepared to go on naked?" Stella inquired, completely serious.

I wished I hadn't retracted the swords.

Pressing my lips together for a hot sec, I decided to keep going. Honestly, I was getting confused myself. "Yes. And that would have been dreadful for the entire production. The reviews would have sucked."

"Musical or straight play?" Irma inquired.

I reminded myself that patience was a virtue and maiming my friends was bad. "A straight play."

"Is this Broadway or community theatre?" Jonny asked as he materialized.

"Does it matter?" I snapped. "The point is that I'm a forty-year-old former child star who has a once in a life-time shot at making a comeback in showbiz. I've known about my Demon heritage for a few weeks and I am in no way prepared to be the Demon Goddess. It's a disaster waiting to happen. The job is waaaaay above my pay grade and I'm not one to pretend I can do something I can't."

"I call bullshit," Cher bellowed. She pulled a wine cooler out of her Prada tote-bag and sucked it back in one gulp. "We're gonna have to agree to disagree on that one. You, Cecily Bloom, can fly! I saw it with my own eyes. Yep, you might have concussed yourself, knocked out a few teeth and needed stitches, but you DID IT! You're a goddamned actress—a genius one. You pretend for a living. I should know, I make ten percent of your income. Your talent gives me a woody and I don't have a cock. If you say you're the Demon Goddess of the Darkness, I'll pay good money for a ticket to the show. I believe in you."

I squinted at her. "Are you wasted?"

"Just a little," she admitted sheepishly. "However, my words are true."

I groaned. "I can't do it. Trust me, none of you want me to do it. I am not the Bitch Goddess Cecily. I'm just Cecily Bloom."

At first, there was silence. Silence wasn't the reaction I was looking for. Preferably, it would have been someone jumping into the scene and telling me I was correct. However, after the stomach-churning silence, there was laughter.

Tons of laughter.

Loud, boisterous laughter.

Tears leaked from their eyes, and my idiot audience rolled on the ground unable to control themselves.

I wanted to electrocute all of them.

I didn't.

The only people who were not guffawing were Dagon, Man-mom, Uncle Joe, Sean, Abaddon and Lilith. Honestly, that was more alarming than the laughter.

I glanced around and winced. We were in full view of my neighbors. Not that I knew any of them, but the grenades, the punching, the purple fire swords and Sushi's fangs were enough for someone to call the cops.

"This isn't a safe place for all of us to show our true selves," I said.

"The entire street is warded," Ophelia reminded me. "Actually, a full half-square mile is warded. Neither Pandora nor her flaming assholes can get to us."

"Not what I'm talking about," I replied. "I have human neighbors."

Fifi grinned and took a bow. "Not anymore, my liege Bitch Goddess Cecily."

"Oh my God," I choked out, feeling light headed with horror. "Did you fornicate with the entire neighborhood and suck out their life force?"

Fifi slapped herself in the head and I almost threw up. "Why didn't I think of that?" she lamented. "That would have been so much quicker and less expensive."

"What are you talking about?" I demanded.

Again, Ophelia stepped in. "Fifi bought every single house in the warded area. She overpaid to get them to leave immediately."

The news was shocking but way better than if she'd banged the neighborhood to death.

"Actually, that was smart. We can house part of our army here for protection," Abaddon said, nodding at Fifi. "I'd be happy to refund the expense."

"Absolutely not," Fifi said, offended. "It's a gift to my liege Bitch Goddess Cecily."

I wasn't sure how all of this was happening, but I was going to improv my way through it. "Can we house Cher, Irma, Moon, Stella, Corny and Jonny here as well?" I asked. Ophelia and Fifi were already my neighbors.

Yet again, I'd confused everyone.

"You're the boss," Dagon said with a kind smile. "Whatever you say goes."

I blew a raspberry. "I work better in an ensemble," I explained.

"As you wish... Bitch Goddess Cecily," he replied with a bow of respect before turning to Fifi. "Please find homes for the Demons and the Angel."

"Will do," Fifi said, saluting Dagon. "I think it would be prudent to have a neighborhood picnic this evening. An informal get-together where we try to avoid violence."

"I can whip up a hotdish," Moon Sunny Swartz volunteered.

Ophelia's eyes narrowed. "What does that mean?"

Moon cracked her knuckles and glared at Ophelia. "It's Tater-tot Casserole, beeotch."

"Ohhhhh!" Corny Crackers squealed. "I love Tater-tot Casserole! Do you use cream of mushroom or cream of chicken?"

Moon rolled her eyes. "Only a jackhole would use cream of chicken in Tater-tot Casserole. Everyone knows that you mix up cream of mushroom, sour cream, milk, garlic powder, dry mustard, a shit-load of shredded mild cheddar and some salt and pepper."

Fifi was shocked and intrigued. I was grossed out.

"My stomach growls for such a delicacy," Fifi announced, offering Moon a grenade. "But I'm confused. Where are the Tater-tots in the culinary masterpiece?"

Thankfully, Moon passed on the grenade. I was going to have a conversation with Fifi about her offering everyone explosives.

"Not to worry," Moon assured Fifi. "The next step is adding ground beef to the mix with some veggies. I like cauliflower, jalapenos and creamed peas. Once you mix that shit up you put it in a casserole dish and layer the Tater-tots over it then liberally—and I mean liberally—spread the shredded cheese over it. Bake it for thirty minutes at four hundred degrees and voila, you have some good eats."

"Yes!" Ophelia shouted. "Bring Tater-tot Casserole. I'm mostly sorry for being bitchy about it."

"Everyone shall bring a dish," Fifi announced. "If you're not skilled in the culinary arts, then bring alcohol."

I had a bad feeling there was going to be a bunch of wasted Immortals after the potluck. How in the hell had I gone from saving my dad to holding my dead mother in my arms to getting schooled on food that contained cream of mushroom soup, cauliflower, jalapenos and Tater-tots in the same day? Sucking my bottom lip into my mouth so I didn't scream, I turned around and faced the woman who bore me and whose job I unwillingly inherited. "Can we talk? Inside?"

She smiled and held out her arms to me. I ran to them willingly and hugged her. It felt so good.

"I love you, Cecily," she whispered against my hair. "Everything happens at the right time. Trust that and trust me."

"Doesn't seem like I have much of a choice," I said with a laugh that sounded tinny to my ears.

"Ohhhhhh, my darling niece," Uncle Joe said, floating down so we were face to face. It was far better to be eye-to-eye than eye-to-wrinkled nut sac. "You may not control all the events that happen to you, but you can decide not to be reduced by them."

I smiled at the clothing impaired ghost. "Maya Angelou."

"Correct!" he said with a giggle. "And… may your choices reflect your hopes, not your fears."

"Nelson Mandela," I said. "But what if it's not my choice?"

Sean took my hand and placed a few sticky green gummies in it. "Choices are the hinges of destiny."

I had to think for a moment on that one. There was no way I was ingesting pot right now, but I hated not knowing the author of the quote. "Pythagoras?" I asked.

"Bingo, sis," he said with a grin. "And one more for the road. You can't make decisions based on fear and the possibility of what might happen."

I knew that one. "Michelle Obama."

"Brilliant and beautiful," Man-mom said, caressing my cheek.

As out of control as my life was careening, it felt strangely wonderful to be with my dad, mom, brother and uncle.

"I've got one," Ophelia announced.

"Should I be scared?" I asked with a laugh.

"Terrified," she assured me with a middle finger salute. "We all have three choices in this shitty life. Do it. Don't do it. Or, do the fuck out of it."

"I'm going out on a limb and taking a guess who said that," I told her as she grinned like a fool. "That's an original Ophelia."

"Bingo, bitch," she replied. "I'd highly suggest you do the fuck out of it."

"Noted." Before I had the chance to ask, Abaddon was by my side.

"Shall we go in and get down to business?" he asked.

If we were alone, I would have thought he meant something else. We were not alone.

"Yep. I suppose if I'm going to do the fuck out of it, I should figure out what doing that entails."

The double entendre wasn't missed by the Demon who had my heart. His grin was as naughty as my thoughts.

Those thoughts would have to wait.

The Bitch Goddess Cecily was about to be born.

CHAPTER THREE

"THERE ARE NO STUPID QUESTIONS," ABADDON SAID SOFTLY AS we followed the group into the house.

"What are you implying?" I asked with a raised brow.

He smiled, tucked my hair behind my ear and pinned me with an intense gaze. "It's not a game to win, Cecily. It's not a TV show. This is your life."

"Which *is* the name of a TV show," I pointed out.

He was confused. The Demon wasn't up on pop culture or TV, for that matter. My joke fell flat. It was irrelevant. He was correct, and I was all ears. The enormity of the situation was beginning to sink in. It didn't feel good. I'd wanted an Emmy, not an army of Demons at my disposal.

"It's so lovely in here," my mom said, glancing around. "You have a beautiful home, Cecily."

"Thank you," I replied. It was lovelier with her in it.

My house was my haven. I'd purchased the Craftsman bungalow about fifteen years ago and Sean had purchased the one next door with the money we'd made from the TV show we'd done as children. My dad hadn't spent a dime of what Sean and I'd made as kids. He'd invested for us. My brother, as an adult, took over the investment job and made all of our money make even more money. Between my jobs, Man-mom's art and Sean's smarts we were ridiculously comfortable for several lifetimes.

Man-mom lived with my brother, but I was pretty sure he'd be finding his own place now that my mom was back in the picture. In this moment, though, my cozy little home was as close to perfect as it had ever been. Man-mom and Lilith sat on the sage-green couch hand in hand. They kept stealing glances at each other and grinning. Their love was so obvious it punched me in the heart.

Sean whipped up some nachos as Uncle Joe supervised and made sure none of the ingredients were expired. Dagon leaned against the wall, his arms crossed over his massive chest. I fidgeted nervously on my favorite overstuffed chair. Abaddon sat next to me on the arm. We weren't touching, but he was close enough that I could feel the heat of his body on my skin. His presence was the calm in the midst of the storm called my life.

Fifi and Ophelia were giving a tour of all the houses my insane bodyguard had purchased and letting everyone pick their new homes. Having Irma Stoutwagon, Moon Sunny Swartz, Stella Stevens, Jonny Jones and Corny Crackers for neighbors was just one more turd pond I'd have to swim around. As much as I'd grown to like them, living by this bunch was going to present challenges. However, I had no one to thank but myself. I'd requested it. And there was no way in hell I would take it back. They'd helped me save my dad from Pandora's psychotic clutches. My strange posse wasn't safe until the stinky whore was back in the box... whatever the box actually was.

The box existed. Pandora said it did. I was going to find it and put her vicious ass in it if it was the last thing I did. I pushed the thought aside because it made me nauseous. Letting my mind race with too many what-ifs was going to paralyze me. Right now, I needed to ask questions. The answers might leave me in the fetal position on the ground, but knowledge was power, according to Sir Francis Bacon.

"Dagon, I'd like you to choose a house in the neighborhood," Lilith said.

He nodded in respect. "If that's acceptable to the Bitch Goddess Cecily, I will do so."

I'd already stated that I work better as an ensemble, but no one seemed to have gotten the memo. Instead of reiterating my stance, I simply nodded.

"Excellent," Lilith announced. "I'd suggest we get down to business then."

"I quite agree," Abaddon said.

"No time like the present," Dagon chimed in.

The fact that everyone was acting like this was normal almost made me laugh. Pretending was for TV and movie sets. I wasn't about to act like I wasn't freaked out and ready to go into hiding.

"Mmmkay," I said, wiping the sticky green residue from my palm due to the gummies my brother had gifted me. I thought about licking it, but Sean liked them strong. Being even slightly high right now wasn't a great plan. I focused on my mom. "I'd like to point out that you died earlier."

"Yes," she agreed.

"But you're not dead."

"Correct," she replied with a laugh. "But I'm no longer Immortal. I'm human with just a dash of Demon."

My dad was almost bouncing in his seat. While that was sweet, it didn't help.

"Look," I said, running my hands through my hair and hoping I had wiped all the pot off my palms. The last thing I needed was sticky hair. My life was sticky enough. "This is a *really* bizarre situation. Expecting me to take over your job is going to end badly. I'm forty. I barely have any experience being a Demon." I looked around the room and paused. Someone was missing. "Wait. Where's Shiva?"

I'd sent Shiva to my home from Lilith's safehouse to help protect my brother before I'd saved my dad. I wasn't too fond of the Demon, but we'd come to a semi-truce when she'd given me the makeup products to help me defend myself from Pandora. She'd banged Abaddon in the long ago past and she wasn't thrilled I was in the picture now. Shiva had messed with me but I'd put her in her place... violently. Now she wanted my ex-husband's digits. Weird didn't even begin to describe that ask. He was a pig. Shiva was on my "wait and see list." Lilith and Dagon trusted Shiva. I'd taken their lead even though I was still a little iffy on her.

"She's with Candy Vargo looking for Pandora," Lilith said.

I sighed with relief.

Candy Vargo was the Keeper of Fate. The crazy woman was fond of toothpicks and four- letter words, but she'd also put the bad in badass. I'd be terrified if she was after me. Candy Vargo had put Pandora in a time-out, so to speak, after she'd abducted Abaddon and tried to destroy him and me. Unfortunately, Pandora had escaped, kidnapped Man-mom and did her best to end my life. Luckily for us, she'd failed and committed the most heinous sin she could have. She'd killed my mom—the other Goddess of the Darkness. I wasn't sure how she could hide from this crime, but the D-List bitch was clever.

"Any news on that?" I questioned.

"Not yet," Lilith said tersely.

Not what I wanted to hear, but it wasn't unexpected. "Let's get back to… umm… *business*," I said with a hollow laugh I couldn't hold back.

My mom got up from the couch and joined me in the over-stuffed armchair. It was a little crowded, but her physical touch helped.

"What do you think the Goddess of the Darkness does?" she asked.

I arched my brow. "I was kind of hoping you'd clue me in."

"And I will," she assured me. "I just want to hear what you think first so I can help you deal with your fears."

It wasn't unreasonable. Closing my eyes, I tried to make sense of the tsunami brewing in my brain. Not possible. "Not sure where to begin."

"Speak from your heart, Cecily-boo," Man-mom suggested.

"Oh yes, darling!" Uncle Joe agreed. "Speak from the heart to be heard."

"William W. Purkey," I said, noting the author of the quote.

My dead, semi-transparent and buck-naked uncle gave me a thumbs up then struck a John Travolta dance pose from *Saturday Night Fever*. It was so wrong it was right—just like my title, Bitch Goddess Cecily.

"Okay, fine. From the heart... I'd like to begin with the fact I'm freaking terrified. I don't want to live in the Darkness. I like my house. I like my life and my friends. Killing people isn't my forte, and I'm sure I'd suck at it if it was on the daily agenda. Unfortunately, I've done a lot of permanent head removal lately, and it worries me that I don't feel shitty about it. Granted, I eliminated flaming assholes who were trying to end me, but something sits kind of wonky with me about that." I sucked in a deep breath and kept going. "Sitting on a big fiery throne in the Darkness sounds painful. Even though I have dark hair, I sunburn easily. Plus, the only time I've been to the Darkness, I was sure I was on a drug trip."

Once I got going, my word vomit wouldn't stop. The sunburn thing was kind of lame, but whatever. Making sense wasn't happening. Abaddon had said there were no stupid questions. I hoped that applied to statements as well.

Standing up, I began to pace. "I never went to regular school because of the TV show. I wasn't on the Student Council, so I lack governing and people skills."

"Umm..." Lilith's eyes were large and she appeared confused.

"I've never even had a pet," I interrupted. "So I think putting me in charge of a bunch of Demons would be an enormous mistake. Also, I'm not remotely religious so I would think that's a strike against me as well. What I really want to do is star in a TV show, bang Abaddon after the appropriate amount of dating and possibly get a kitten." I slapped myself in the head. "Actually, I'm not sure where that came from. I don't want a cat. And I really don't want to be the Bitch Goddess Cecily."

"Cats are lovely animals," Uncle Joe announced. He was on the floor doing yoga. The visual was bad.

"But you *do* want to bang Abaddon?" the man in question inquired with a grin that made my knees weak.

"Fuck. I said that out loud?"

"Yep," Sean replied with a laugh as he tossed me a baggy filled with gummies. "You're killin' it, sis. Try the orange one. It's mild and might calm you down."

I did as he suggested and chewed up the orange gummy. It couldn't get much worse. I'd already announced to my parents that I wanted to get sweaty and intimate with the Demon known as the Destroyer. "I would surmise after my unhinged monologue that none of you would want me to take over Lilith's job."

"May I speak now?" Lilith asked with a slight wince and a crooked smile.

I sucked my bottom lip into my mouth and nodded.

"Okay. First, that was a lot," Lilith said, trying and failing to suppress her grin. "Second, let's go over it point-by-point and address your concerns."

"Oh my God," I muttered, hoping the gummy kicked in quickly. I wasn't even sure what I'd said.

My mom continued. "It's smart to be scared. Means you have a healthy sense of self-preservation, something you need in this job."

I squinted at her. "I think you might be reaching."

"Stay with me," she said with a chuckle. "Being a Goddess is your birthright. What you need to be a Goddess is already inside you. You've proved it multiple times already. Even when you were scared, you refused to back down when Abaddon was in danger. You stopped Fifi from nuking Corny. You saved your father without a thought for your own safety."

"Those are people I care about."

"You made sure that Irma, Stella, Moon, Corny and Jonny didn't get killed by Pandora—you protected them," she reminded me. "You didn't like them at all."

She kind of had a point there, but anyone with a shred of decency would have done the same. Plus, I liked them now.

"Parents don't always see their kids in a rational light," I pointed out. "Rose colored glasses and all…"

She ignored my comment and kept addressing my concerns. "You don't have to live in the Darkness. Very few actually reside in the Darkness."

"Wait," I said, perplexed. "You don't have a castle and a moat and all that kind of stuff?"

"Actually, she does," Dagon said.

Lilith shot him a stern glance. "I have a large home in the Darkness because grandeur makes my people feel more secure. Most of the time I reside in the safehouse you visited."

"Seriously?" I asked.

"Very," she replied. "That being said, the palace is now yours. However, you may continue to live here."

"And spend holidays in Hell?" I asked, making sure she wasn't hiding anything.

The question threw her. I was good like that.

Lilith shrugged. "I suppose if you want to. Although, the Darkness isn't all that big on human holidays."

"Got it," I said, slightly embarrassed. It might be better to listen and not talk for a bit.

"A Demon Goddess never kills unless it's in defense of her people or herself," Lilith explained.

"Guess Pandora missed that memo," I said, unable to stop myself.

"Amongst others," my mom agreed flatly. "On to your other concerns. The throne isn't made of fire, so your ass is safe."

"Oh! Thank goodness for that!" Uncle Joe said.

Lilith giggled. I was surprised she could hear Uncle Joe, but she still had a slight glow around her.

"Cecily does *flame* to please," Sean added with a mouthful of nacho.

"Very punny," I muttered. "I'm not sure if that was sweet or gross."

"Me either," Sean agreed with a chuckle. "Can you tell I'm a sitcom writer and a poet?"

"Nope," I replied, tossing the bag of gummies at him.

It was hard to believe how incredibly normal our inter-action was considering the conversation being had.

"More, please," I said to Lilith.

She obliged. "I'm not sure what a Student Council is, but I assure you that Dagon and Abaddon will keep you apprised of the laws."

"Demons obey laws?" I asked, feeling skeptical.

My mom patted the space next to her. I joined her on the chair.

"The short answer to the question is yes. However, sometimes Demons must be convinced to abide. But… the most important factor is that things are rarely as they seem," she said. "What would you expect the Grim Reaper to do?"

"Is this a trick question?"

"Not at all," she said.

"Take bad guys to Hell," I replied, picturing my Uncle Gideon the Grim Reaper in my mind.

"Wrong," Dagon chimed in. "That's the job of the Angel of Mercy."

"Daisy?" I asked.

I'd only met them twice, but they were clearly kind of scary. Well, not Daisy, but definitely Gideon.

"Dagon is correct," Abaddon said. "Most souls have already determined where they will reside in the afterlife by the way they lived their human years. However, if there's a soul in question, that's where the Grim Reaper and the Angel of Mercy come in."

"It was decreed that way from the beginning of time to avoid conflict of interest," Dagon supplied. "It's not often that it happens, but when it does, the system has been set."

I nodded. I had a lot of preconceived notions that I was probably going to have to drop kick out of my head. "I guess I've always thought that Demons are bad and Angels are good."

"Bullshit and fiction," Cher grunted as she entered the house with a wine cooler in each hand. "Angels are some of the worst sons of bitches I know. And I should *know*."

My inebriated and overly made-up agent was an Angel. A fact I'd learned recently when she removed her shirt and downy white wings burst from her back. To say it was alarming would have been an understatement. However, she'd saved the day. Green lipliner or no, Cher usually saved the day.

"What are we yacking about?" Cher asked, taking the bag of gummies out of Sean's hand and putting them in her bottomless purse.

"We're discussing how crappy I'll be as the Bitch Goddess Cecily," I told her as she plopped down next to my dad.

"You're more than qualified, oh, Favorite Client of Mine. How about I show these people how you can fly?" she asked, pulling a laptop out of her bag.

"How about no?" I said quickly, grabbing the laptop and tucking it under my ass. I'd destroy it later. Knowing Cher, she had a backup, but I'd deal with that too. I didn't need anyone in the room to see my twenty-year-old self getting humiliated on camera for a kid's show I didn't even book.

"Alrighty then," Lilith said, getting back on track. "As to your other concerns, organized religion is the doing of humans. There have been more wars fought over religion than you can shake a stick at. It's an oxymoron, and it doesn't concern us. Heaven and Hell are more abstract than real. We refer to it as the Darkness and the Light. But honestly, all of it is gray. There's very little in the Universe that's black and white."

"True that," Cher said, pulling a twelve-pack of wine coolers out of her bag and setting them on the coffee table. "Drink up, people."

"It's the middle of the day," I pointed out.

"Five o'clock somewhere," she shot back with a cackle as she popped the top on a bottle.

My mom, always polite, took a wine cooler and joined Cher. "As to what you want to do with your time, you can do the TV show. Being a Goddess doesn't preclude you from having a life. There will have to be more protection because Pandora's still at large, but I think it's a grand idea to follow your dreams. Most choices we make are the right ones if we're doing them from a place of passion or love. Also, cats are lovely and complicated creatures. I believe you'd do well with a cat. I know just the one for you. As to the rest…" She gestured between Abaddon and me. "You'll have to work that one out with each other."

"Way to dodge, Lilith," Sean said, holding up his hand.

My mother did not leave him hanging. She slapped the offered high-five and laughed. "Thank you, Sean."

If you can't beat them, join them. I grabbed a wine cooler and slugged back a gulp. "Okay, you've addressed my unhinged diatribe. Now I want to know what I have to do if I take the job."

"It's not a matter of accepting it or declining it," Lilith said. "It's already yours. You were born into it."

I inhaled deeply and exhaled slowly. "What if I fail?"

"Only those who dare to fail greatly can ever achieve greatly," Man-mom said.

I couldn't believe we were playing the quote game, but at the same time, it was perfect. "Robert F. Kennedy."

"Bingo," Man-mom said. "What have you got?"

I smiled. I knew what the old man was doing, and I was going to dive right in. "The greater the obstacle, the more glory overcoming it."

"Moliere," Sean said, pumping his fists over his head. "Try this one on for size... Our very survival depends on our ability to stay awake, to adjust to new ideas, to remain vigilant and to face the challenge of change."

"Martin Luther King Jr.," I replied, feeling less terrified than I had a half hour ago. "I can do this!"

"Yes you can, mother humper," Cher announced, raising her bottle high.

I laughed. It was better than mother f-er.

Lilith put her wine cooler down and took my hands in hers. "The goal is peace. The obstacles will be many. Demons can be a violent species. However, they want to live in harmony like any other being. To help them accomplish that, you must accept change. You must seek support and focus on the goal not the obstacles. Embrace your failures as much as you celebrate your wins. Most importantly, you must be as compassionate with yourself as you are with others and stay humble. Pride is the sin that destroys."

"More specific directions would be nice," I said. "You know, like examples."

Lilith laughed and kissed my cheek. "One step at a time, darling child. Deal with what's in front of you and always make your decisions with forethought and compassion. You did it not even ten minutes ago."

I looked at her in surprise. "I did?"

"You did," she confirmed with a naughty smile. "I was exceedingly proud of you that you didn't decapitate Moon after hearing the ingredients in Tater-tot Casserole."

I wasn't sure if it was because the gummy had kicked in or if it was my mom's wildly irreverent sense of humor, but I laughed. Hard. For five minutes.

I wasn't convinced that I was the right gal to be the Goddess, but, apparently, the choice wasn't mine to make. It simply was. My DNA made it so. According to Bette Davis, 'The key to life is accepting challenges. Once someone stops doing this, he's dead.'

I had way too much to live for. Bette Davis and I were on the same page.

CHAPTER FOUR

THE SUNSET WAS STUNNING—BLAZING ORANGE AND PINK.
The purple bougainvillea crawling up the walls of my little
house shimmered in the light. While the air in LA could be
smoggy, living close to the ocean was a treat. All I could
smell was the salt from the water and the light scent of
lemon coming from my trees. The calm I felt was due to
many things at the moment... the hangover effects from the
gummy Sean had given me, the two wine coolers that Cher
had insisted I drink, my mom and dad holding hands and
sitting on my porch swing and Abaddon by my side.
However, the majestic beauty of nature's work was in stark
juxtaposition to what was going down on my street.

Tables and chairs had been set up on the road in front of
my house. I wasn't sure how they got their hands on
balloons and six life-sized cardboard cutouts of David
Hasselhoff, but I kept forgetting my buddies possessed
magic... and seriously weird taste. The crowd consisted of

inebriated Demons, Succubi and a very tipsy Angel. I was shocked and thrilled that no one had lost an appendage... yet. It still boggled my mind that Immortals could regrow arms and legs. Of course, someone had shown up with a cornhole board and beanbags. Irma and Ophelia had almost come to blows over whether cheating was permitted. After a bunch of threatening and posturing, they decided if someone cheated and didn't get caught it was fine.

I came close to stepping in and banning cheating, but Dagon had suggested letting it go. He told me to wait for bloodshed before putting my foot down. Crazily, the Demon made sense. Or maybe I was just crazy. Although, when Fifi suggested playing cornhole with grenades, I ended that shit quick.

"You have to try this," Ophelia insisted, shoving a bowl of what looked like vomit at me. "It's fucking delish! Moon is whackadoo, but the bitch can cook."

"Nope, I'm good," I said, holding up both hands in defense of myself against the Tater-tot Casserole. I could do a lot of things. Eating what looked like a dog had puked it up wasn't one of them.

"You're missing out, bitch," she informed me as she wandered away singing Moon Sunny Swartz's praises for her culinary masterpiece that I would definitely call a shitshow.

I milled around and chatted with my new and old friends. Sean was having a blast talking poetry with Dagon, and Uncle Joe was holding a dance contest on my lawn. Corny had worked up a sweat twerking. It was terrifying to watch. Sushi and Stella were comparing boob jobs. Jonny was hitting on Fifi. I sincerely hoped nothing came of that since Fifi was a Succubus and sucked the life force out of her paramours. She'd sworn she'd been celibate for four hundred years. I expected her to keep her streak. I'd keep an eye on the situation. Jonny wasn't the sharpest tool in the shed, but he'd grown on me like a non-deadly fungus.

Sadly, it occurred to me that Jenni wouldn't be able to be part of this strange and somehow wonderful crowd. She was one hundred percent human. Jenni had been on *Camp Bite* with me and Sean all those years ago. Sean and I had played vampires and Jenni was our bubbly human counterpart whose catchline was *Holy Moly! What would Dracula do?* She'd left the business after the show ended, went to cosmetology school and was now one of the most sought-after makeup artists in Hollywood. She was my lead hair and makeup on *Ass The World Turns*. My heart hurt at the thought of having to hide most of my life from my BFF, but it was probably best for her safety and sanity.

"Hey!" Cher yelled, sitting at one of the picnic tables. "Come sit with me, Bitch Goddess Cecily. We need to talk shop."

My agent was fairly wasted, but I decided to hear what she had to say. Abaddon laced his fingers with mine, and we walked together to the inebriated Angel.

"So," Cher began, propping her tiny stiletto-clad feet up on the table and giving anyone who wanted a nice view of her bright pink panties. "I say we get *Ass The World Turns* up and running. Every dang studio in town is trying to beat us to the punch with an over-forty female comedy aka a miracle midlife series. It would chap my nethers to a bloody pulp if we got squashed by some suit-wearing, MBA, pencil pushing turd-knocker. You feel me?"

"Dude," I said with a wince. "Your choice of words is nasty."

She grinned. "Make 'em love you. Make 'em hate you. Never let 'em forget you."

Cher was unforgettable. I chuckled and shook my head. "I'm a little concerned about the cast now."

My agent's eyes grew huge. "What in the Hell's Angels are you talking about? We got the best of the best. Aubrey Zawn, Janie Stone, Sammy Sam Samuelson and Wanda Adams are the best in the biz."

"They're human."

Cher looked at Abaddon. Abaddon looked at Cher. They both started laughing at the same time. I was completely left out of the joke.

"Umm... would someone like to clue me in here?" I asked, getting annoyed.

"Not human," Cher said, still laughing. "Not a single one of them."

"Shut the front door," I shouted. "Are you serious?"

"No. I'm Cher. But yes, I'm serious," she said.

I had to pause for a hot sec and replay her answer in my head. Cher could be confusing when she was sober. She wasn't sober.

"Are they Demons?" I asked.

"Sammy, Aubrey and Janie are Angels," Abaddon explained. "Wanda Adams is a Demon through and through."

"Well, Ophelia did say that Hollywood was loaded with

Demons," I muttered, reaching into Cher's bag and pilfering a wine cooler.

"Wait," Cher said, perplexed. "I thought you picked them because you knew."

"I didn't even know I was a Demon when I chose them," I told her.

Abaddon raised a brow. "I'd told you that you were a Demon."

I eyed him back. "And I told you to get therapy for your delusions."

He grinned. "Good times."

Letting the fact that I'd inadvertently chosen a demonic and angelic cast was a lot to swallow. "What about the director of photography, Bean Gomez?"

"Demon," Cher supplied.

I shook my head in shock. "The writers—Georgia, Jameson, Rick and Kristen?"

Cher cackled and slapped her thigh, almost upending herself from her chair. "Regular old Immortals."

"Bitch Goddess Cecily," Jonny called, looking wildly put out.

"Crap," I said as he marched over in a tizzy. I checked him over quickly. Thankfully, he was alive and in possession of all his body parts.

"I need to speak to you," he ground out.

"Yes?" I replied.

"In my opinion, I do believe I'm being made fun of," he huffed. "The problem is, I'm not sure. BUT, if those beeotches over there are pulling my leg, I shall remove theirs."

I glanced over at Abaddon. He shrugged. I guessed this was a Goddess thing.

Jonny was super handsome and lacking in the brains department. Back in the day, he'd been fond of the words, babe, guy and 'in my opinion.' His *opinions* left everyone open-mouthed in confusion.

Years ago, I'd done a crappy informercial with him for a knock-off version of Transformers. Instead of the robot turning into a cool car, it was a possessed-looking doll that turned into a flowerpot. It had been taken off the market when customers complained that the crotch of the demonic doll was too anatomically correct. I'd had nightmares about that job for months. However, the gig had paid great. Jonny had been a diva then and was still a diva.

"Mmkay," I said. "Tell me what happened."

He glanced over his shoulder and flipped off Irma, Ophelia, Fifi, Stella and Moon. They were laughing hysterically. That didn't bode well for the gals keeping their legs.

"They made me say words then they lost their idiot shit minds," he snapped.

"What words?" I asked, knowing full well I didn't really want the answer.

"Mike, who, cheese, hairy," he told me, throwing his hands in the air.

I was now as confused as Jonny Jones. Abaddon didn't get it either.

Apparently, Cher did.

"You gals are naughty," she yelled to the giggling group.

I squinted at my agent. "Wanna share what's so funny?"

"Say it," she insisted gleefully.

"Mike. Who. Cheese. Hairy," I said, clueless. "Still don't get it."

"Say it all together and fast," Cher instructed.

"MikeWhoCheeseHairy," I said, then choked out a horrified laugh.

Jonny was livid and began to glow. The potluck was about to end in dismemberment. I quickly grabbed Jonny by the arm and pulled him down next to me.

"If you chop any legs off, I'm going to be pissed," I warned him.

"What they said was disgusting," he hissed. "Firstly, I don't have a cootchie. And if I did, I'd wax it."

"TMI," I said with a wince. "The best way to get them back is to play them at their own game."

"Not following, Bitch Goddess Cecily."

"I can help you with that," I promised.

"On no," Abaddon muttered, scrubbing his hands over his handsome jaw.

"Oh, hell yes," Cher said.

"Explain," Jonny said, still pouting.

Demons were such a sensitive bunch. "Repeat after me. Dang Lin-Wang."

He grinned and repeated.

I nodded my approval. "Now say these ones. Peter Pantz. Anita Bath. Betty Humpter. C. Mike Crack."

Jonny recited the names and trembled with excitement.

Abaddon's head hit the table with a thud. "How old are you? Twelve?"

"I'm forty and fiiine," I shot back. "Even you have to admit, a little potty talk is far better than a bloodbath."

"Fine point. Well made," he conceded. "Remind me to stay on your good side."

"Will do," I said as Jonny sprinted back to the gals, screeching their new monikers.

Of course, Ophelia was no slouch in the profanely insulting names department. We'd had a go of it on a long car ride to Vegas. When I'd heard her call Jonny Anita Fartinghouse, I'd lost it. At least they were having fun, and no one was bleeding. It was the little things that counted.

"Houston, we have a little problem," Cher announced with a gag.

Quickly, I turned my head in the direction she was looking. Relief washed over me as I realized it wasn't a life-threatening issue. It was just foul and alarming.

Uncle Joe had been a nudist in life. He was a nudist in death. I was getting used to it. My uncle was one of my favorite people in the world—sweet, kind and adorable. My fondest wish was that he'd stick around for a while. He loved flying, dancing, yoga and making sure the food in Sean's and my houses wasn't growing fur or mold.

Corny, on the other hand wasn't nearly as cute as my uncle. Two decades ago, I'd done a movie of the week with him. He'd played my dad. Off camera, he'd hit on me repeatedly. It was disgusting. Twice I'd been treated to the visual of his wrinkled junk. I had my dresser steal his dentures to get the old man to back off. I'd refused to give them back until I had it in writing that he'd sexually harassed me and would never bother me again. He knew I'd go straight to the tabloids if I had to, which would ruin his nice guy persona.

It had been before the Me-Too movement, when jackasses like Corny didn't see anything wrong with exposing their ding-dongs to women on the regular. The pilfering of the dentures had been genius. The idiot hadn't wanted the world to know he was toothless. I'd dipped them in the toilet before returning them. It was the little things that created the most joy.

The movie we'd done had stunk. My character, Miranda Diamond, had moved back home from the big city to help with the failing family Christmas tree business called the Bush Bonanza. The matriarch of the family had passed on in a bizarre gardening accident that was referred to constantly but never explained. That was bad, but it got worse.

Much to my own personal horror—not Miranda's—I'd given up my swanky, high-paying job in NYC, came home and fell in love with a lumberjack/ horticulturist who didn't speak English. Dolph Gunter—played by a guy whose name I couldn't recall. No one could explain the oxymoron of his jobs… He was supposed to be German but sounded more like The Swedish Chef from the Muppets. He'd also had some seriously bad breath and there had been far too many kissing scenes. I'd refused to watch it when it aired. Sean and Man-mom had thought it was hilarious. It wasn't a comedy.

Suffice it to say, the Demon was an idiot, but he'd stepped up in a major way to help me save Man-mom. For that, I would let his past be his past. One of the Demon's gifts was flying. He'd helped all of us avoid getting offed by Pandora. Unfortunately, he flew best while naked.

The dance party on the lawn was over. Corny Crackers

and Uncle Joe were now flying around and squealing like little girls.

Naked.

Both of them.

It was one thing to see a ghost naked. It was entirely another to see a flesh and blood Demon's junk flapping in the wind. Again, I was glad I hadn't partaken in the Tater-tot Casserole. It looked like poop in a bowl. I couldn't begin to imagine what it would look like being hurled out of my mouth.

I groaned. "Is that really my responsibility?"

Cher winked. "You're the Bitch Goddess Cecily, and that buck-assed naked geezer is one of your people. So… I'm gonna have to say yep."

"Shit," I grumbled and I stood up. "This is getting ridiculous."

I refused to look up and see the underside of their balls. Marching over to the tree where they were perched, I looked straight ahead and spoke in my outdoor voice. Sadly, I faltered and glanced up. Their wrinkled testicles swayed in the breeze. I seriously wished mind bleach was a real thing. "Corny, what the hell do you think you're doing?"

"It's thrilling!" he shouted. "I had no clue that you lived in a nudist colony. It's my dream come true!"

I ran my hands through my hair and considered my options. Making Uncle Joe feel bad about his *natural* life choices wasn't on the table. Body parts were body parts. I reminded myself that bodies of all shapes and sizes were beautiful. It was problematic to see Corny's naked body as beautiful, but I was going to find a way… or throw up trying.

"Actually, this isn't a nudist colony," I said, doing my best to stay diplomatic. "Not sure where you heard that rumor." I wanted to say I was too old for this crap, but realized most of the people here had several thousand years on me.

The weird was real.

Corny began to cry. I felt awful.

"I am so sorry, Bitch Goddess Cecily," he sobbed as he dropped from the tree and landed in a nude pile at my feet. "I've never fit in anywhere. Always the bridesmaid, never the bride."

"Umm…" I wasn't sure what to do with that analogy.

Corny got to his feet and hung his head. "I'd also like to apologize for flashing my junk at you all those years ago. I did it to prove to the world I was a real man. I assumed—which made a laughing stock and an ass out of me—that my secret would be safe if I touched women's bottoms and displayed my wiener in public."

"Not following," I said. "How would that keep the fact that you're a nudist safe?"

Uncle Joe floated down from his branch and patted Corny on the back. His ghostly hand went right through the Demon, but the gesture was kind. "Dear Corny's secret wasn't that he prefers to live in the buff," he explained.

I got it fast. My heart broke for the strange old Demon.

"Corny, there's nothing wrong with being gay," I said softly.

Corny wiped his tears, then picked up a few leaves and blew his nose. "Back in the golden days of cinema, it made one a pariah. My agent made me swear to keep my sexuality a secret."

"Who in the fuck was your agent?" Cher bellowed. She was furious.

"Chucky Bucky," Corny admitted.

"Chucky Bucky's a fucking asshole," Cher snarled. "Got busted for skimming residuals off his clients to the tune of ten million. Pecker's in jail now."

Corny was shocked. "Really? I didn't know. He dropped me eight years ago. Told me I was an untalented old fruit."

"Who's your agent now?" Cher demanded, slapping her hands on her hips.

The Demon blanched. "I don't have one."

"You do now, you naked nut-job," she shouted pulling papers out of her ever-present Prada bag. "I'm your fucking agent. However, you're gonna have to wear clothes when you go on auditions."

"I can do that!" Corny assured her.

On hearing the news, Stella Stevens, Irma Stoutwagon, Jonny Jones and Moon Sunny Swartz sprinted over and dropped to their knees in front of my tiny badass agent. Ophelia and Fifi hung back. Cher had already signed them.

"Please, oh great one with the green lips," Irma begged. "Please take me on as a client too."

Cher was a bit confused. She pulled out a compact mirror, checked her lips and screamed. Corny offered her the snot-covered leaves to wipe it off. She declined.

"You mother humpers need to let me know when I've lined my lips with a fucking eye pencil," she complained as she pulled tissue out of her bag and scrubbed at her mouth.

"I will do that," Stella swore. "If you take me on as a client, I'll barnacle myself to you and slap you every time you make your lips green... or blue... or charcoal."

"That's a little much," Cher commented.

"I'd be happy to service you daily if you sign me," Jonny offered, flexing his muscles and giving Cher his thousand-watt smile.

My agent rolled her eyes. "I don't dip my pecker into business, dumbass."

"Do you actually have a pecker?" Moon Sunny Swartz asked.

"Nope," Cher said with a laugh. "But I do have big lady balls. Can any of you act?"

They all exchanged worried glances. No one said a word. So much for my little posse having any self-confidence.

"I've offered all of them roles in season one of *Ass the World Turns*," I admitted.

"That might have been good to know," Sean commented with a wince as he joined the group. "As your head writer, that's kind of important."

I gave him an apologetic smile. "It was kind of a spur-of-the-moment deal. However, they were all part of some of the worst job and audition stories I've experienced. I think we can make it work."

"Oh yes!" Corny gushed. "We've also been told if we suck, we only get one season."

Sean was speechless and just nodded politely. He smiled at the new cast members, popped two gummies and wandered away.

Cher was not speechless. She rarely was. Pulling

contracts out of her purse, she handed them out. "Sign them. All of you are good-looking. If your acting stinks, we can set you up with print work. What I say goes and if any of you give me flack, I'll kick your asses into next year." She glanced around then narrowed her eyes at Moon. "Didn't I rep you for five minutes years ago?"

Moon paled and nodded. "Yes. You umm... fired me when I put a snake in your toilet."

"Jesus H. Christ," Cher said, shaking her head. "You're a fucking menace."

I jumped in. "Moon's working on her impulse control. She hasn't humped furniture on a set in years." My defense wasn't terrific, but I couldn't think of anything else.

There weren't a whole lot of positive things to say about Moon as far as her behavior on TV shows. She was basically un-hirable in Hollywood. The certifiable gal was known for playing pranks on set. From what I'd heard, she had nine restraining orders against her.

I'd done a TV pilot with the whacko eleven-ish years ago called *Roommates*. Basically, it was a ripped-off version of *Friends*. Moon had been caught in a *prank* getting jiggy with the furniture on the set during lunch break. The couch hadn't survived. Unfortunately, the debasement of the furniture had been on the same day the studio heads were watching the show. She'd recorded her performance and put it on the internet. It had gone viral. The show didn't get picked up. It hadn't been that great of a sitcom, but Moon humping the armchairs and everything else in sight had been the nail in the coffin for that production.

"You're on probation," Cher informed Moon as she

handed her a contract. "If I find any reptiles in my house or if you get jiggy with even one inanimate object, I'm done. You feel me?"

Moon grinned and saluted her new agent. "Roger that!"

"Cecily," my mom said, walking over to the newly signed clients of Cher. "I believe we should have a conversation with Corny. I think it would be prudent. I have a hunch he can help."

Corny shrieked with delight.

I had no clue what she meant, but I wasn't second guessing her. "Now?"

"Now," she confirmed.

"It would be my honor," Corny said, bowing to both of us.

"Let's take this inside," I suggested. "Follow me."

I didn't know what was about to go down, but I could do it or I could not do it. Or I could do the fuck out of it.

I'd decide the right course of action, once I found out what *it* was.

CHAPTER FIVE

"CORNY," I SAID IN THE POLITEST WAY I COULD. "IF YOU'RE
going to sit on my couch, you need to put on some underpants. Bare asses are not permitted on the furniture."

"Except mine, because I'm dead," Uncle Joe let everyone
know.

He got a round of applause.

"Listen to the boss, Corny," Ophelia warned. "Skid
marks on a sofa is gross."

My thoughts exactly. I just wanted to be a little less blunt
about it.

"Good thinking!" Corny agreed. "Do you have any
boxers I can borrow?"

"For real?" I asked.

"Yes."

"Jesus Humperdick Christ," Cher grumbled as she dug
though her purse and produced a pair of men's boxer-briefs.
"I don't want them back."

"Thank you, Cher," Corny said, stepping into the undies before getting comfortable on the couch.

His bare butt had touched it, so I was still going to have it steam cleaned. Hell, now that he was my neighbor I would have to invest in plastic slipcovers.

"Shall we get started?" Dagon inquired.

"We shall," Lilith said.

"Bitch Goddess Cecily and Lilith, how may I be of service?" Corny asked.

While my house wasn't tiny, it wasn't what I would call large. With all of us piled into the living room, it was a bit tight. Didn't matter. Lilith had requested that everyone join in. As far as I was concerned, her word was the law. I might be the Goddess, but she was my mom.

"I'll let you know shortly, Corny. First, it's story time," Lilith said as she stood up and addressed the Immortals in my den. "But a question before we begin. Who can tell me what they know about Pandora's box?"

"Her vagina?" Fifi asked.

"Okay, nope," I cut in quickly. "Not a vagina, a literal box."

"But is it?" Stella asked. "Is it truly a box? I've always heard it was more of a vessel."

"Pottery?" I questioned. Stella, Jonny, Irma, Moon and Corny had at one time been loyal to Pandora. They'd broken away from her evil clutches and had been surviving in the Demon world on their own for centuries. One of the conditions that Pandora had made to let them leave was that they could not show loyalty to Lilith. Her demand had left them alone and unprotected in a violent world. It wasn't until I reluctantly agreed to be their Goddess that they were part of a family again, so to speak. They were now mine whether I wanted them or not. The truth was I did want them. They were a handful, but they were good deep down.

"Not sure about the pottery thing," Stella admitted. "I think it's more abstract than something tangible."

"I've heard a rumor it's not a box or a vessel," Irma chimed in.

"Did the rumor include what it actually is?" I pressed.

"No."

We were getting nowhere fast. Hopefully, Lilith would have more constructive information.

"There are many interpretations of Pandora's box," Sean commented. My brother wasn't a Demon, but he was badass smart. "The human understanding from Greek mythology is that it's an artifact. It's referred to in Hesiod's 700 BC poem, *Works and Days.*"

Lilith's eyes sparkled with genuine warmth at my brother's response. She was enchanted by Sean. Duh. Everyone was. He was a special kind of awesome. "Go on, Sean," she insisted.

Sean gave her a thumbs up. "As the poem goes, Pandora's curiosity led her to open the box or vessel that was in her husband's care—given to him by the Gods. In doing so, she released curses on mankind—sickness, death, and other undefined evils. When she tried to close the box, there was one single thing left behind that didn't escape. Hope. Extremely ironic and tragic. Of course, in modern times, opening Pandora's box means creating a shitshow. Or more specifically, playing with the unknown can lead to a catastrophic chain of events that will spin our world into chaos."

"Excellent," Lilith said, patting my brother on the head. "Aptly put. So smart. Just like your father."

Sean grinned and offered her a gummy.

She declined. "Storytime," my mom said. "What the humans know about Pandora's Box has some veracity to it, but the truth is far darker."

"Catastrophic chain of events that will spin the world into chaos is pretty freaking dark." I shivered involuntarily.

Abaddon put his arm around me and pulled me close.

I leaned into him, enjoying the comforting warmth of his body against mine, then nodded to my mom. "Can you be specific?"

The Immortals were always so damn cryptic. It drove me nuts. I wanted to scream, *say what you mean and mean what you say*, but I'd been at this Demon stuff long enough to realize it didn't work that way. There wasn't time to argue the merits of clarity at this point. Pandora was on the run and had very little to lose at this point. She'd committed the one crime that was beyond the pale. She and Lilith had ruled the Darkness for millions of years as mortal enemies. Their duo-reign had only lasted because they were forbidden by Immortal law to harm each other.

Pandora fucked that up.

"That's where Corny comes in," Lilith said.

Everyone was confused—especially Corny.

Abaddon cleared his throat and gave the former Goddess of the Darkness a look. She, however, remained unperturbed. Instead, she kept her gaze on Corny Crackers who was sitting on my couch in his, or rather Cher's, underpants.

"I repeat." I pulled on my hair, and strands came free in my fingers. Great. Stress was beginning to take its toll, and I was going to be Bald Bitch Goddess Cecily if I didn't get it under control. I took a deep breath and blew it out noisily. "I need more specifics, please." Because if she planned to send Corny on his own after Pandora, it wasn't happening. He wouldn't stand a chance.

"It's simple," Lilith stated flatly. "I don't believe Pandora let the evil out of the box."

She hadn't addressed my concern, but her statement was odd. "Is that pertinent?"

She nodded and got a faraway look in her lovely eyes. "In the beginning, the Higher Power set the rules."

All the Immortals in the room paled a bit. Even Abaddon and Dagon.

"God?" I asked, confused.

"No. God belongs to human religion. The Higher Power is more of an entity—an elusive light. Smoke and mirrors— danger, love and wickedness personified. Not something to be questioned or called on. Like I've said before. The Universe is neither black nor white. It's gray. The Higher Power could also be considered gray."

That didn't sound good to me. "Holy shit," I muttered. "Does he ever just randomly show up?"

"The Higher Power is neither a he nor a she. It just is, but that's not the crux of the story," she explained. "The point is that in the beginning, Pandora wasn't evil. On the contrary, she was a good and moral woman."

"What the actual fuck?" Cher demanded. "I didn't know that."

Lilith raised a brow and gave my agent a sad smile. "Not many do. From what I understand it was the Higher Power who gifted the box to Pandora for safekeeping. It seems it may have been a cruel joke."

"What were you given?" I asked, wanting to make sure I wasn't inheriting something shitty and terrifying from the Higher Power. It was enough that I was in charge of Demons.

"A key," she said.

My stomach got a bit wonky. "To the box?"

"Possibly," she said.

Closing my eyes, I wanted to scream. Did any Immortals do things the nice and easy way? It didn't appear that way. "Lay it on me."

Lilith sighed and ran her hands through her wild dark hair that was so much like mine. "I was given words and told they were the key. I was never told what the key opened, but it's possible it's for the box."

I waited for more. There was always more.

"The truth can shift. In the Darkness, the seed of hope awaits. Behind every smile lies a dark and tragic secret. What you see is rarely the whole truth. Some bridges are meant to be burned. And embrace what is repugnant to discover the beauty that lies beneath. Often the answer has been in front of you the entire time."

I memorized the words. I might not know what the heck I was doing as the newly appointed Bitch Goddess Cecily,

but I was one hell of an actress and could memorize like
a pro.

"Got it." I stood up and walked over to the window. The sun
had gone down and the evening sky was full of stars. Normally,
I would wish on the first star I spotted. Not tonight. I needed to
make my own luck. "How is Corny involved in the story?"

"He spoke of the Tome of Dark Magic earlier," Lilith
answered. "I believe the secret to Pandora's box are in the
pages of the book."

"You've never seen the book?" I asked.

"No," Lilith confirmed. "In the beginning, it was
bequeathed to both of us and stolen by Pandora."

"And it's caused untold issues over millions of years,"
Dagon said in a tight and furious voice. "Bloody, deadly and
unnecessary issues."

I blew a raspberry. "Why didn't you tell on her?" My
back was to the room, but I felt all eyes on me. Ignored
everyone else as I turned to face my mom. "Why didn't the
Higher Power do something about that? If it was meant for
both of you, why didn't the thing in charge make it right?"

Lilith, perplexed by my questions, answered with
silence.

Abaddon shook his head. "While logical, that's not how
it works. The gifts are given. How we deal with them is
on us."

"I call bullshit on that," I muttered.

"Bitch Goddess Cecily," Dagon said. "With all due
respect, Lilith refused to fight in order to avoid
Armageddon."

"Isn't that from the Bible?" I asked. My knowledge of religion was limited, however, even I knew that Armageddon was biblical. "Is the Bible an accurate history?"

"That fucking part of the book is accurate for the most part," Cher chimed in. "Always tickles me pink that the Four Horsemen are drag queens."

I was pretty sure that wasn't in the Bible, but what did I know? Nothing, apparently. Even though my curiosity was piqued, I decided to stick to the Tome of Dark Magic instead of the Bible. I was a Demon, after all.

Honestly, I couldn't believe how all these people lived as long as they had. It seemed the modus operandi was to trust some invisible meanie aka the Higher Power. This gray blob who embodied danger, love and wickedness. Some jackhole who'd thought it was smart to give the deranged woman a bunch of evil in a freaking box and let her steal the sacred book. And to the nice Goddess the blob gave some words that made very little sense. Pressing the bridge of my nose, I decided to be logical. I'd think of it as a one-hour drama. By the end of the episode, we needed to solve the case and put the bad guy—or woman—behind bars.

"Corny," I said, pointing at him. "Have you seen the book?"

He nodded. His expression looked like he had sucked the juice out of an entire a bag of lemons while constipated.

I wasn't done. If he puked on the floor, he was cleaning it up. "Do you know where it is?"

"Many moons ago, I saw it in the Darkness. In Pandora's palace," he whispered.

Corny and crew hadn't been loyal to Pandora in

centuries. The chances of the book still being there were slim, but it was the only lead we had in the maddening puzzle. I glanced over at Abaddon and Dagon. "Is it possible to get in there and steal it?"

Abaddon's head fell back, and he stared at the ceiling. Dagon stared at the floor.

I rolled my eyes. "I'm in charge. Right?"

"Darn f-ing tootin'," Cher agreed.

"As I see it, if the skanky bitch isn't caught, we're all in danger—especially Lilith. Pandora takes no issue with killing humans, even though it's technically off-limits for Demons. Her goal will be to destroy me without killing me." Of course, killing my mom had been off-limits as well, but that hadn't stopped her. "Maybe. She might be so unhinged at this point she won't care about the rules set by the gray blob."

"Who?" Ophelia asked, confused.

"My bad," I said. I finger quoted my next words. "The Higher Power."

"Jesus Herman Christ," Cher choked out. She pulled out the bag of pot gummies she'd pilfered from Sean and popped a few. "I'm going to suggest you refrain from calling it the blob."

"Noted," I replied, moving on. "I need Candy Vargo's number. I want updates on the search for Pandora. The next item on the agenda is that I want Lilith, Man-mom and Sean to go to the safehouse. I need them out of harm's way. I want full protection there to guard them. I can't do what I need to do if I'm constantly worried about their safety."

"As you wish, Bitch Goddess Cecily," Dagon said.

"I know you have a lot of supernatural crap happening right now, Sis, so I feel like a shit asking this, but are we or are we not doing the TV show?" Sean asked.

I had to mull that one over for a sec. If I was going to die, I was going down doing something I loved. "Are," I confirmed. "You can zoom with the writer's room and we'll talk every day. I have no clue why we're doing that show considering what's going on, but my gut says yes. I'm following my gut."

He gave me a two-finger salute. "Works for me."

Lilith didn't look as certain. "You need me and my knowledge. I should be here with you."

"I don't disagree," I told her. "But I also need you alive. You already died in my arms once. Not sure I'd live through a repeat. Besides, that's what phones are for. You can drop any knowledge I might need in a text message. Besides, any of the Demons guarding the safehouse can relay messages to me if, for some reason, the phones don't work."

"Lilith, Cecily is right," Man-mom said, taking her hands and pressing his forehead against hers. "If our daughter is worried about our safety, it could mean she disregards her own. That's a hard no for me. We're all aware that Cecily will go to the ends of the earth for those she loves."

My mom kissed my dad sweetly on the lips, then turned to me. "It's a little difficult not being in charge," she said with a small laugh. "But you're correct… Bitch Goddess Cecily." She shook her head and smiled at my Goddess name.

I smiled back. It was left of center, but so was I.

"Pandora went after you to destroy me," she continued.

"She will go after me to destroy you. Your plan is excellent. Once you find the book, I will help you decipher it."

It was embarrassing how close I came to squealing. I might have preened just a little at my mother's approval… "Thank you. I love you, Man-mom and Sean. Losing you again after I just got you back would be worse than death."

"We should go now under the cloak of darkness," Dagon said. "I shall transport the three of you."

"And I'll call in back up for protection. They will be there when you arrive," Abaddon added. He snapped his fingers and produced three glowing cell phones and a laptop. "Use these. They're undetectable and can't be traced."

Sean put the electronics in his man purse and then shook Abaddon's hand. "Take care of my sister," he said in the most serious tone I'd ever heard my brother use. "If you screw up or hurt her, you'll have to answer to me. And, yes… I am *fully* aware that you could kill me with a flick of your pinky finger, but I won't go down without getting a few damned good punches in and a solid knee to the testicles."

"Sean Bloom is the sexiest man alive," Fifi bellowed, saluting my brother. "While I imagine him naked often, I would never screw the life force out of him. Sean Bloom makes the world a better place."

None of us were sure what to do with that, so we did nothing. Sean reluctantly saluted Fifi back with a terrified expression.

Jonny Jones and Stella Stevens stepped forward and bowed.

"It would be an honor to guard your family," Jonny said. "I believe that my gift of invisibility might be an added layer of protection."

"And my tits are something no one sees coming," Stella added with great pride, pointing at her perky girls. "Legendary. I would also be humbled to protect your family."

"What do your tits do?" Cher asked.

Stella began to remove her shirt.

I stepped in quick. "How about we tell, not show?"

The insane woman giggled. "Good thinking, Bitch Goddess Cecily. It would be unfortunate to riddle the walls of your home with bullet holes."

"Jesus Hyrum Christ," Cher cried out. "Your knockers are guns?"

"Machine guns," Stella said. "They also dance."

Before she demonstrated the boob dance, I quickly accepted the offer. "My answer is yes. I would be grateful and pleased if you would aid in the safekeeping of my family."

"But you idiots will miss being on the TV show," Irma pointed out.

Jonny didn't miss a beat. It surprised me. "There will be more TV shows. There is only one Lilith, Man-mom and Sean."

My mouth dropped open. There was way more to Jonny Jones than met the eye.

"I also will be earning brownie points with the Bitch Goddess Cecily and will be superior to all of you. With my good looks, killer smile and six-pack abs, I'll be a revered Demon. I would surmise it will be easier to get laid."

Ahh, there was the Jonny I knew.

"What he said," Stella added.

I wanted to laugh. I didn't. Their magical gifts were so bizarre they might very well come in handy. However, I wasn't going to let Jonny be a dick. "There are no brownie points to be had. My eternal gratefulness will have to suffice."

"I can work with that," Jonny confirmed. "But I would like everyone to acknowledge that my fuckable potential will increase."

Like Uncle Joe getting applause for reminding everyone that it was fine for his naked ass to be on my couch since he was dead, Jonny also got applause. I didn't join in. My people were certifiable.

I extended my hand to Dagon. He shook it with a bemused expression. It wasn't the norm for a Goddess to shake hands with her people, but there was a new sheriff in town who'd only known of her Demon heritage for a few short weeks. My human side was showing, and I planned to keep it that way. Shit was going to change. Lilith said to embrace change. That was going to have to go for everyone. "Please transport them."

He bowed.

Man-mom grabbed me and hugged me tight. My dad was a distracted mess of profound wisdom. He was absent-minded. He was loving, and he gave the best hugs in the world. Sean and I had grown up with unconditional love. It was a true gift. I held on to my dad and rested my head on his strong shoulder. I'd almost lost him. I was pretty sure the enormity of that hadn't hit me yet. The truth was I didn't have time to dwell on what happened yesterday. The goal was to focus on the now and make sure Man-mom was safe. It was bound to hit me eventually, but it would have to wait until Pandora was back in her mysterious box.

Sean was next on the hug list. I was impressed with his warning to Abaddon. My sibling's joy for life was undeniable. His penchant for pot, poetry, yoga and playing the stock market made him one of a kind.

We hugged, and he kissed the top of my head. "Do the fuck out of it, sis."

"Will do," I promised as my eyes got watery.

Lilith cupped my face with her slim hands and kissed my nose. "You're everything I dreamed of and more. It was from afar, but I have loved you with every fiber of my being since the day you were born. Listen to Dagon and Abaddon. They will never lead you astray. Nor will I." She wrapped her arms around me and held me close.

The feeling was unexplainably perfect—far better than all of my childhood dreams. I no longer blamed her for abandoning me. She had no choice, and I would have done the same in her position. Lilith loved me enough to leave me. She loved me enough to die for me. My dreams had shifted from anger to acceptance and love. My fervent desire now was for her and my dad to live the rest of their lives in peace and joy.

That was non-negotiable.

My old motto was, *let's get this party started*. My new motto was, *do the fuck out of it*. I planned to do exactly that.

CHAPTER SIX

"REPEAT THE BULLSHIT YOU JUST TOLD ME ON THE PHONE," Candy Vargo demanded. The woman was glowing, and her eyes were narrowed to slits. She was wearing ratty sweatpants, an inside-out sweater vest, and mismatched shoes. It was terrifying... all of it.

"Pandora killed Lilith. Lilith is human," I quickly replied. "I'm the new Goddess of the Darkness." I took Abaddon's hand to steel my courage. While I was pretty sure she wasn't irate with me, Candy was fond of property destruction first, talking after. I loved my house. If she blew it up, I'd be pissed.

Candy Vargo's mouth was wide open. Her toothpick had fallen out. She didn't even pick it up and put it back in her mouth. That was saying something for her.

"Get the fuck out of town." The foul-mouthed Keeper of Fate dropped down on my couch right on top of Uncle Joe.

My dead uncle simply floated right through her then seated himself across the room. "You can't be serious. You don't know shit about being a Goddess of Darkness."

Her lack of confidence in me wasn't what I needed right now. I was doing a fine job of not believing in myself all on my own.

Ten minutes ago, I'd called her for an update on the whereabouts of Pandora. She asked me to explain what the actual fucking fuck was going on—her words not mine. I did... kind of. She kept interrupting. I kept trying. The Keeper of Fate shouted a litany of swear words then hung up on me. She showed up in my living room exactly three seconds later. Scared the heck out of me. I wasn't used to people just poofing in surrounded by shimmering dust.

"Didn't Shiva get you up to date?" I asked warily.

Steam was coming out of Candy's ears. I'd never seen anything like it in my life. Even Abaddon appeared concerned. His eyes turned a bright red and his jaw worked furiously. If the Keeper of Fate and the Destroyer got into it, my house was a goner. Hell, all of California would prob-ably be a goner.

Putting my hand up, to let Abaddon know I could handle it, I waited for an answer from Candy.

"That demonic idiot, Shiva, talked a mile a minute. Said Lilith was dead, then said she wasn't. Confused the fuck out of me," Candy grunted. "Kept babbling her fool head off, so I electrocuted her to calm her ass down, but I was a little too enthusiastic."

"Oh my God," I gasped out. "Did you kill Shiva?"

"Nah," she assured me. "She just needs to grow back a

few body parts and the bottom half of her face. Not to worry, Gideon is healing her. She'll be fine."

I puked in my mouth a little.

"Candy Vargo," Cher shouted, waggling her finger in the glowing woman's face. "You need to relax your damned crack and quit incinerating people who are not the bad guys."

"Up yours, Cher," Candy said, flipping off her long-time friend. "And just for your information, I'm taking fucking anger management classes."

Cher raised an expertly plucked brow while rolling her eyes. "And how's that going?"

"Obviously not well," Candy snapped.

I shook my head and sighed. "Okay, how about we stay on track here? I need to know if there are any leads on finding Pandora?"

Candy took a deep breath and calmed down. "The short answer is no. However, I need to know exactly what happened with Lilith."

I obliged. It took forty-five minutes. By the time I'd finished getting her up to speed on what happened with the battle and the aftermath to my mom, she'd chewed through two boxes of toothpicks. The coffee table and the floor were littered with tiny pieces of wood. I was impressed she didn't choke to death.

There was a good five minutes of silence while Candy digested what I'd said.

"What Pandora did is punishable by death—death as an Immortal and death as a human," Candy ground out.

"That would be a grave mistake," Abaddon cut in. His

tone was as cold as ice, sending a shiver up my spine. "The balance would be permanently destroyed."

"Like it's not already?" Candy countered in a tone that matched Abaddon's.

"Stop. Stop it right now," I said in my outdoor voice. "I have enough junk going down without you guys maiming each other or worse. We're all on the same team here." Both Immortals had the grace to look ashamed. That was a relief and gave me a bit more confidence. I kept pushing my own agenda. "What do you know about the Tome of Dark Magic?" I asked Candy.

"Not much," she admitted. "Heard of it, but never saw it. Why?"

"Lilith believes the secret to Pandora's box are in the pages of the book." My mind began to race with millions of questions. It hit me like a ton of bricks how much I didn't know. "Do you have more toothpicks?"

Candy grinned. "Always." She tossed me a box. I popped one in my mouth and chomped down. It was bizarrely comforting. "We need to backtrack."

"How far?" Abaddon asked.

"Umm… unclear," I admitted with a laugh that sounded like I was on the edge of losing it. Since I was, I went with it. "How many Demons am I in charge of?"

"Right now?" he asked, cagily.

"It's not a trick question. Why do you sound so weird?"

He ran his hands thorough his hair and exhaled loudly. "The straight answer is, I don't know. Most of our people are unaware of Lilith's demise."

"Kind of sort of demise," Ophelia corrected him.

Abaddon silenced her with a look. He was terrifying when pissed. She slunk back behind Fifi and Sushi.

He continued. "We'll do a formal announcement. Word is most likely spreading as we speak. We'll need to go into the Darkness and you'll have to stake your claim."

That didn't sound good at all. "Will that be bloody?" I whispered.

"I hope not," he replied.

Sometimes the truth sucked.

"More questions," I pressed.

"Ask," he said.

"How many are loyal to Pandora?"

"Numbers will not be helpful right now," Abaddon shot back flatly.

I wanted to scream. I wanted to electrocute him. Instead, I turned to Fifi. "The house across the street—is anyone living in it?"

"No, my liege Bitch Goddess Cecily," Fifi said.

"What the hell did she just call you?" Candy Vargo asked with a laugh of disbelief.

My patience was wearing thin. The feeling of drowning in the overwhelming reality of what my life had turned into was making my head spin. Yep. I knew Candy could blow me to smithereens with a wave of her hand, but I didn't care.

"My name. You gotta problem with it?" I demanded, leveling her with a stare that was either going to earn me some respect or end me. Right now, I'd be fine with the second option.

She threw her head back and cackled. "Badass!" she bellowed. "I always said you were a badass."

Looked like I was going to live for at least another few minutes.

"Excuse me," I said, walking out of my house and across the street. I was well aware that everyone was watching me from the windows of my house. Didn't matter. I'd learned from the Demons that property damage was cathartic. I'd proved the theory to myself when I'd destroyed the exercise equipment in the fight training room back at Lilith's safehouse.

It was time to put the theory to the test again. I was so wound up, I needed to exorcise a few demons. I laughed hard at the irony of my thought. My audience would think I'm crazy.

I was.

But I was going to own my crazy and deal with it in the best way I knew how. No one had batted an eye when I'd blown apart the training room. Honestly, it seemed like pretty normal behavior for demonic whack jobs. And since I'd joined the whack job club—albeit unwillingly—I was going to take advantage of the perks.

Eyeing the house, I felt a thrill run through me. "Fifi," I called out.

"Yes, my liege Bitch Goddess Cecily?"

"You're positive this house is empty?"

"On the life of my secret love, Sean Bloom, I swear it is indeed empty," she promised.

"Umm… not really a secret," I muttered under my breath.

Even so, I inhaled the lemon-scented breeze and went for it. Wiggling my fingers then slashing my arms through the air, I detonated the adorable Craftsman house. The loud boom as the house exploded made me hope that the magical ward around our neighborhood would muffle the sound. It was gnarly to watch it burn. However, I had to admit I felt less stressed. Property destruction was cleansing.

"You done, motherfucker?" Candy yelled from my front porch, grinning from ear to ear.

"Just getting started," I informed her as I marched back across the street and into my house.

"That's my badass," she said, smacking me on my backside and sending me flying.

Abaddon caught me. His amusement was evident. He winked and kissed me soundly on the lips. It made me tingle and forget about the horrible task ahead of me for all of ten seconds. Dragging him back to my bedroom and forgetting about life for a few hours sounded like heaven.

Heaven would have to wait.

Moon Sunny Swartz bowed low then bounced up and down like she had to pee.

"You have something to say?" I asked.

"I have a plan," she squealed.

"Jesus Homer Christ," Cher mumbled. "Does anyone need a valium?"

I almost said yes. "What's your plan, Moon?"

"It's genius," she replied as she lovingly stroked my favorite overstuffed chair and began to rotate her hips.

"If you hump my chair, I'll electrocute you," I told her.

"Roger that," she said, quickly moving away from the piece of furniture. "So, do you wanna hear it?"

"No, but that's never stopped me before," I said. "Tell me."

CHAPTER SEVEN

IT TOOK MOON ALL OF THREE MINUTES TO SPEW OUT HER plan. She spoke fast—very fast. There were several points where I was sure I'd misunderstood her, but from everyone else's expressions in the room... I hadn't.

It took ten minutes of silence to take it in.

Abaddon paced back and forth. I had no freaking clue what the man was thinking. Several times he opened his mouth to speak then thought better of it and continued pacing.

Fifi and Sushi whispered with each other. I had a very good idea about what the two Succubi were discussing, considering the roles Moon had in mind for them in her *plan*. Cher found some white wine in my kitchen, and poured everyone a glass before drinking the rest straight from the bottle.

Irma and Ophelia were just shocked, but seemed to be leaning towards a yes.

Only Corny and Uncle Joe were nonplussed. They were discussing the difficulties of being a nudist if one loved hiking. Honestly, Moon's proposal was so far out there, I'd much rather discuss how to keep my privates safe from mosquitos and the dangers of wiping one's ass with poison ivy.

No such luck. I had to deal with the *plan*.

I liked some of the plan, but most of it was flat out ridiculous. I understood Abaddon's dilemma. Every time I tried to give an intelligent reply nothing came out of my mouth.

Candy didn't have any problems speaking up. "That's the most fucked up shit I've ever heard," she said, picking her ear with the toothpick that had been in her mouth only moments earlier. "I think it might just work."

Moon screamed with joy. In her excitement at being complimented by the Keeper of Fate, she began to seduce my couch. It was not a pretty picture. She got a few good humps in before she got cock-blocked, or couch-blocked, rather violently by a powerhouse right hook from Ophelia before getting drop-kicked across the room by Irma.

Between Corny's bare ass on my cushions and Moon's lewd attempt at banging the sage green sofa, I was done. Next week, I was buying a new couch.

"You know…" I said, deciding diplomacy was overrated. "Having the Succubus army bang the lives out of all of Pandora's followers isn't working for me. At all."

"It's fucking absurd," Abaddon muttered. "No pun intended."

"Hang on," Candy said. "Let's go over this bullcrap. One,

you need the Tome of Dark Magic to figure out how to get the bitch back in the box. Correct?"

"Correct," I replied.

"Two, you have to go to the Darkness anyway to claim your Bitch Goddess Cecily status."

"True," I agreed.

"The underpants fucker, the one who dropkicked the couch humper and the couch fucker herself are the only ones familiar with Pandora's castle. Right?"

"Right."

Candy scratched her head then pulled out a clean toothpick. She tossed it in the air and caught it in her teeth. "The Succubi thing is a little whacked, but it would definitely get the point across that you're in charge now."

I winced. "I'd like to do that without forcing the Succubi to have sex with a bunch of Demons and, as a byproduct, killing an ass-load of people." I wasn't sure which would be worse, feeling like a pimp or being responsible for mass murder.

Candy nodded. "I get that. Never good to start with a bunch of blood on your hands. However, we're talking about the scum on the bottom."

"No," I corrected her. "We're talking about people. People like Underpants Man, Dropkicker and Sofa Fucker." I slapped myself in the forehead. "I mean Corny, Irma and Moon."

"Not to worry, Bitch Goddess Cecily," Corny assured me. "I quite like Underpants Man."

"Ditto," Irma said. "I'm cool with Dropkicker. Nice ring."

"Couch Fucker is accurate," Moon announced. "But if I

may be so bold as to suggest Sofa Shagger or Sofa Schtupper? The alliteration makes it more memorable."

Candy deferred to me on that one. The huge grin she was sporting was too much. I flipped her off. She returned the favor. Most people feared the Keeper of Fate.

I adored her.

"Moon, you can choose which one you like best. I think all of them are... umm... graphic."

"I'm going to tell you something right now," Cher butted in. "If you legally make that shit your legal name, I'm dropping you as a client. There is no way in hell I'm repping someone named Sofa Shagger."

Corny raised his hand. "What about Underpants Man?"

"Nope," Cher informed him. "Corny Crackers is strange enough. I'd rather have my bottom lip pulled over my head than rep a man's undergarment."

"I see how that might not appeal," Corny told her with a thumbs up.

"I think Dropkicker might be better than Irma Stoutwagon."

That revelation made everyone pause.

"I don't know about that," I told her. "Irma Stoutwagon is hard to forget."

"I agree," Candy Vargo stated. "It's badass in a nerdy way. I love it. Irma Fucking Stoutwagon."

Irma preened under Candy's praise.

"Irma Fucking Stoutwagon it is!" she shouted.

Cher elbowed Candy in the gut so hard the toothpick flew out of her mouth and across the room. She glared at Cher, but got the message.

"Just Irma Stoutwagon," Candy corrected herself much to Cher's relief. "The f-bomb will limit your potential for Hallmark movies."

"I love Hallmark movies," Irma gushed. "They're brilliant, deep and they make me horny. I would be perfect as city girl high-powered CEO who inherits a Christmas tree farm from a long-lost relative, so I decide to sell it off and put all the farmhands out of work until I fall in love with the grumpy caretaker and, finally, fulfilled as a woman, I quit my high profile, high paying job with a pension and benefits that I went to six years of college and ten years of hard work to earn so that I can bake sugar cookies and pop out babies for the rest of my life with the man I love."

My eyes widened. "Moving on," I said, before we began to debate Irma's very specific love of cheesy romance. "Somebody help me understand the layout of the Darkness. Are Lilith's and Pandora's castles close to each other?"

"It's not that simple," Abaddon said. "You can't think in a linear way or with human logic."

"Not helping," I told him.

Abaddon stood as still as a statue. His body went rigid, and shimmering black sparkles popped and crackled around him. For a hot sec, I wondered if he was still alive. When he finally moved, everyone in the room except Candy jumped.

The man kept talking as if he hadn't just seemingly turned to stone. "Figuring out the geography of a place that's an illusion of sorts is an exercise in futility."

"Same with the Light," Cher commented.

Abaddon took my hand and led me to the couch. I

refused to sit on it. He realized why immediately and grinned. I loved his smile. He smiled more now than when I'd met him. There was still pain in his eyes, but I liked thinking I made it easier for him. It was kind of bold since we were just dating... but we were both aware it was far more than that.

We'd get to us eventually. I led him to an overstuffed chair, pushed him down and sat on his lap. "Explain it to me in a way I can understand."

He nodded and pulled me close. His scent was delicious and made me lightheaded. For a beat, I forgot we weren't alone. The Demon could make me forget my own name.

"In the Darkness, you go by what your gut tells you. I'll be by your side, but it's a matriarchal society. Only you will matter to them."

"How will we gather everyone so I can stake my claim?" I asked, then made a face. "And how exactly do I stake my claim?"

"It's never been done, so I'm not sure," he replied. "You just go with your gut. It's worked for you so far. As to how you get your people there... you'll call to them, and they will come."

I groaned. "I'm more of a rehearsal kind of gal. Improv isn't my thing."

"Make it your thing, motherfucker," Candy Vargo said. "We need to get that evil Demon into her box. I figure if we lock her up for a few hundred fucking centuries, she'll have some time to think about the crimes she's committed. The sooner, the better."

Sushi walked over to the chair and sat on the arm. I'd

known Sushi for decades. We'd worked together multiple times. She was a top-notch costumer in the biz. Her impeccable wardrobe design had won her a few Emmys and an Oscar nomination.

My friend was blunt with a sarcastic sense of humor and crazily talented, but I recently learned she was also the ten-thousand-year-old Queen of the Succubi. The species of Immortals who, when having sex, ended the lives of their paramours.

To say that was shocking was an understatement. The Succubi under her reign were working on celibacy. Sushi had sworn off sex nine centuries ago. She'd gotten depressed about killing all her lovers. She traveled with a vibrator to take the edge off.

She grimaced. "While I'll go on record and say that Moon Sunny Swartz is batshit nuts..."

"Thank you," Moon said in all seriousness.

"Welcome," Sushi replied. "I think she might be onto something by having my people help you."

I squinted at her. "You're cool with your people banging Pandora's people into oblivion?"

She shook her head. "No. Not at all. It would set us back hundreds of years. However, one of the points Lilith made was to accept change. You have to accept change and so do your people. You can be the Goddess who brings together all the species."

"Still not following," I told her. "Are you there as backup to screw the lifeforce out of Demons if they're not into change?"

"I don't think it will come to that," she said with a

chuckle. "Just the sight of a thousand or so Succubi standing with you might encourage them to behave."

I mulled it over. Something didn't sit right. Abaddon's body tensed beneath mine, but he didn't say a word. Slowly, I slid off his lap and circled the room. The scene wasn't going to work as written. If I went to the people who were supposed to trust and follow me with an army of another species ready to fornicate them into nonexistence, that would end in chaos and fury. My gut told me so, and apparently, I was supposed to listen to it. Lilith only threatened her people when they defied her. I wanted them to love and trust me like they did my mother.

However...

"I'm doing a rewrite on the scene," I said.

"This isn't a TV show," Abaddon reminded me, pressing the bridge of his nose.

"Nope, but I'm an actress and this is how I make sense of things," I told him. "Stay with me here." He nodded, so I continued. "I like the slant of including other species. It's probably past time that we all get along. But, and it's a big but, I only want Cher and Sushi with me along with Ophelia and Abaddon."

"Keep going," my agent said, taking notes with her purple eyeliner pencil. "Liking it so far. It has intrigue with an edge of unpredictability."

That was good. A solid scene led you on a chase to figure out what would happen next "I'm concerned about the safety of Corny, Moon and Irma. I know they're familiar with Pandora's palace."

"In the show I think we should call her Stinky Whore," Moon suggested.

"Oh, and would you be so kind as to use our new monikers?" Corny asked. "It feels more like a real one-hour drama if we're using character names."

When in Crazytown, one must hop off the train and buy a piece of property. I'd arrived and I was committed to staying. "Not a problem. I'm concerned about the safety of Underpants Man, Dropkicker and Couch Fucker. While they know the layout of Stinky Whore's palace, it's been a very long time since they've been there. I'm quite sure they won't be welcomed back with open arms. Better?"

"Can you go with Sofa Shagger for me?" Moon inquired politely.

Polite went a long way in my book even if what we were discussing was insane. "Sure. Sofa Shagger. And I think the way to combat my fear and keep my people safe is to send Fifi and an army of Succubi with them. I'm pretty sure Pandora's flunkies aren't going to want to get into it with individuals who can snuff them out with sex."

"One thousand individuals," Sushi added with a curt nod to Fifi.

My self-appointed bodyguard pulled out her phone and began quickly texting.

My stomach went a little wonky that the scene I was making up as I spoke it aloud was about to come to life. I wasn't a writer. I was an actress. However, I'd been punching up shitty scripts for a long time. It would help my sanity to look at the situation as a show in progress. I would rewrite it as many times as needed.

"Should I stay here and hold down the fort, darling child?" Uncle Joe asked, floating over and hovering in front of me.

I smiled at the beautiful man. "Yes. That would be perfect."

"You can't wear that," Cher commented.

"Wear what?" I asked.

"Jeans and a t-shirt," she said. "No one in the Darkness is going to take you seriously if you look like a soccer mom."

"Fuck to the yes," Candy backed her up. "You gotta wear black with high heels that'll pinch your toes and make you hate the world. I'd suggest some side boob as well. Shows you got confidence."

"Side boob shows confidence?" I asked, confused. Candy Vargo dressed like she'd walked out of a dumpster. I wasn't sure I should take fashion advice from her.

"You're a damned dingbat," Cher muttered to Candy as she waved her hands and conjured me up a new outfit.

Gone was my comfortable clothing. I was now dressed in a black sequined Prada gown that fit me like a glove. It was off the shoulder and had a low back. Thankfully, no side boob. The stilettos were going to make me hate the world eventually, but right now they made me feel like a goddess.

"Okay," I said as the butterflies in my stomach wet nuts. "Underpants Man, Dropkicker, Sofa Shagger and Fifi will transport directly to Pandora's palace. Abaddon, Cher, Ophelia and Sushi will transport with me to Lilith's palace."

"Your palace," Abaddon reminded me with a look in his eyes I couldn't quite decipher. What I did know was that it made me breathless. And the butterflies liked it too if their breakdancing in my gut was any indication.

I took a deep breath and dove into the scene with everything I had. "My palace. We will transport to the Bitch Goddess Cecily's palace."

"That's the ticket, motherfucker," Candy Vargo said with a grin. "You're a badass. Be the badass."

"Do you want to come?" I asked, realizing I'd left her out.

"You don't want me to come," she said. "If the Keeper of Fate shows up in the Darkness, the end is fucking neigh."

I gulped. My world had gotten a whole lot bigger and a shitload scarier. I pushed my morbid thoughts aside and stayed in character. I still felt like Cecily Bloom—former child star trying to make a comeback in Hollywood at forty. Bitch Goddess Cecily didn't feel as real to me. Too bad. So sad. I would just go method, and fake it until I could make it. There didn't seem to be any other choice.

Two quotes came to mind. Moliere's 'The greater the obstacle, the more glory in overcoming it.' I was my obstacle. The Demons who I needed to accept me were my obstacle. Pandora was my biggest obstacle. I would overcome them all.

And the other quote was Ophelia's 'Do it. Don't do it. Or Do the fuck out of it.' It was succinct, profane and perfect. I choose door number three.

I glanced around and smiled at my small and powerful posse. I wanted to make Abaddon proud. I wanted to prove to Candy Vargo that I truly was a badass. Mostly, I wanted to make my mom proud.

"Wait," I said, realizing part of the cast was missing. "The

Succubi army. Do they know where we're going? How to find us?"

"Not to worry," Sushi assured me, taking my hand and walking me over to the bay window that looked out on my front yard.

I gasped. A thousand Succubi dressed in white tuxedos and red patent leather shoes stood shoulder to shoulder. They were armed to the teeth and ready to rumble. Upon seeing their queen, they bowed in unison.

"Wow," I whispered. "Thank you."

"The pleasure is mine," she replied. "Fifi, take Underpants Man, Dropkicker and Sofa Shagger outside, please. The Succubi army awaits you."

"As you wish," Fifi said. She handed a grenade to each of the Demons.

I'd seen them fight. They didn't need grenades, but an explosive backup was always handy.

As the quartet left my cozy house, they bowed to me with respect. I nodded my respect back.

Ophelia, Cher, Abaddon and Candy Vargo joined us at the window.

"Holy shit," Ophelia said. "I've never seen so many hot people wearing red shiny shoes in my life. And I've lived a long fucking time."

"Lot of deadly horndogs out there," Candy said with a chuckle.

Cher elbowed her buddy again. "After that anger management course, you're gonna take an etiquette course."

"You and Gram are up my ass all the time," she grumbled.

"Because we love your nasty ass," Cher shot back.

"Let me know when you get back," Candy Vargo said.

"Well, unless you die."

On that shitty note, the Keeper of Fate disappeared in a blast of sparkling orange glitter.

"Are we ready?" I asked.

"Are *you* ready?" Abaddon countered.

"No, but I'm going do it," I said.

Ophelia clicked her tongue at me. "No bitch," she said with a naughty grin. "You're going to do the fuck out of it."

"From your mouth..." I muttered as we joined hands.

"Hang on to each other," Abaddon advised. "It's going to be a bumpy ride."

I didn't expect anything less.

CHAPTER EIGHT

THE TRANSPORT INTO THE DARKNESS, A RIDE SO INKY BLACK I couldn't see my hand in front of my face, sucked. My head pounded, and my skin felt as if it were melting off my body. The roar in my ears was so loud I could barely think, let alone hear. Screaming would've been useless. An arid wind whipped through my hair, and the sensation of falling into an abyss consumed me.

And then, in a snap, it was over.

I opened my tightly clenched eyes and I let out a soft sigh of relief.

A vast mountainous landscape of raging fire lay in front of me. The words wicked and sultry came to mind as I watched the flames lick up the sides of trees bearing strange fruit that made my mouth water. Swarms of large, brightly colored birds soared through the fire. Their wing spans were the width of a four-door sedan, and the crashing sounds they made reminded me of the grate of metal on metal in a deadly pileup of cars. A huge red sun hung low in an inky purple sky.

My breath came in quick spurts, and I felt a strong kinship to the shocking scene. The Darkness looked the same as when I was here last, but it felt very different. Before, I had been a stranger in a strange land. It had felt both unreal and surreal to the point that I'd been certain The Darkness was a drug-induced hallucination. This time, though, I could feel the Darkness coursing in my blood. This time it felt like home.

We stood side by side in the place that was my birthright. Cher gasped in awe. Sushi reacted the same. Ophelia and Abaddon sighed with contentment. I pictured Lilith in my mind to calm my frayed nerves.

Closing my eyes, I went over each and every one of our meetings—from the first time I heard her melodious voice on the phone, and when I saw her looking so young and beautiful in the empty casino parking lot. I shuddered, thinking about the moment when I'd thought I lost her. Holding her dead body in my arms had been soul-crushing. I shook off the cold shiver of dread and pictured my most current memory of her—alive and happy, kissing me goodbye before she and Man-mom left for the safehouse. The vision of her smiling face filled with love calmed my soul.

I could do this.

My mom believed in me. I simply needed to believe in myself.

"What the actual fuck?" Ophelia shrieked. "What's happening?"

Abaddon's animal-like growl made my blood run cold.
I opened my eyes and quickly scanned the area for
danger. Raising my hands, I produced my purple fire
swords and stepped in front of Cher and Sushi. Abaddon
was a killing machine and could handle just about anything.
Ophelia had a good chance of defending herself since she
was a Demon. Cher and Sushi, however, were not Demons.

"What did you see?" I demanded, still looking for danger.
I saw nothing.

"Lilith," she said, completely confused. "I saw Lilith."

"WHERE?" I shouted. Had Pandora kidnapped my
mother and brought her to the Darkness? Could a human
survive in the Darkness?

"There." Ophelia pointed to an empty space right in
front of me. "She's gone now."

The tingling started in my toes and quickly spread
through my body. No one was going to harm my mother.
No one. Especially not Pandora. My body began to spark
and a searing hot fire danced along my skin. A rage boiled
up inside of me I didn't know I possessed. If the Shitty
Whore had my mother, she was going to die by my hand.
She'd already killed her. Wasn't that enough? I no longer
gave a damn about the rules. She was going down for good
this time.

My fury was so intense that flames began to shoot up
around me. My vision turned blurry, and I thought I saw
Ophelia grab Sushi and Cher and toss them to safety. I
didn't look back. Looking back made you lose time. I didn't
have time to lose.

"Show yourself, Pandora. You're batshit if you think

you'll succeed a second time. I am the Bitch Goddess Cecily. You killed my mother. Prepare to die," I shouted. My unhinged laugh when I realized I'd basically quoted Inigo Montoya from *The Princess Bride* was strangely fitting. The fire I'd caused blazed across the already fiery landscape. The intensity sparked a hunger for more as I stoked the flames until they were an all-consuming wildfire. The power of the Darkness was mine to call. I was in my element, and I would burn Pandora alive.

"NO CECILY," Abaddon bellowed. "It's not real."

His voice sounded far away, but I could hear the urgency. Abaddon was my touchstone. He loved me. He wouldn't lie to me. Everything came crashing down on me all at once—my emotions, my fear, my anger. I was losing my mind. So many things that were not in my control were controlling me—Lilith's death, Man-mom's kidnapping, Abaddon being tortured in Vegas, beheading the flaming assholes who had done their best to end me... becoming the Bitch Goddess Cecily.

It was too fucking much. There was only so much a forty-year-old former human could take before she broke into pieces.

"Help me," I cried out as I dropped to my knees.

"Look at me," Abaddon roared. "Now." Strong hands pulled me to my feet and shook me hard, forcing me back into reality.

"Help me," I begged him as flames encircled my body the same way it covered the land around us.

"Control your magic," he ground out. His eyes were wild,

and his face flushed. "I can no longer undo what you do, Cecily. You're the Goddess of the Darkness."

My heart felt like it had lodged in my throat. I shook my head and tried to clear the outrage and confusion.

"You can do this," Abaddon commanded. "You can control your power. You have to."

The quotes from earlier came roaring to the forefront of my mind. 'Obstacles are those frightful things you see when you take your eyes off the goal.' Henry Ford. I was my obstacle. The goal was to claim my place as the Bitch Goddess Cecily. If I blew the Darkness into smithereens, that wasn't going to happen.

The second quote was just as powerful. 'Our very survival depends on our ability to stay awake, to adjust to new ideas, to remain vigilant and face the challenge of change.' Martin Luther King Jr. I was awake, but that was about it as far as succeeding at what Martin Luther King Jr. had suggested we strive for.

Sucking in a huge breath, I made a valiant attempt to tamp back my anger. Lilith had told me anger could be productive unless you let it consume you. I was close to letting it destroy me. Unacceptable. I focused my breathing and slowed my heart rate. The flames began to subside, but I couldn't shake the sense that danger was still close by. "Pandora. Where is she?"

"Not here," Abaddon promised.

"Lilith?" I demanded.

"Not here," he said. "She's at the safehouse." He cupped my face in his hands and raised my gaze to his. "It's okay. It was an illusion. You're okay. I believe you projected your thoughts."

"What does that even mean?" I asked. My heart still pounded like a jackhammer in my chest, but the need to burn the world down had lessened.

"Ophelia," Abaddon called out. "Explain to Cecily what you saw."

Ophelia's voice was ragged and she sobbed through her words. "It was all the past. I saw Lilith in the field right after Cecily beheaded the flaming assholes. Then it morphed to the interior of the theatre in Vegas. Lilith was in disguise. Morphed again. Lilith was in a house filled with fucking scary art with a Hell theme. Then I saw her dead in Cecily's arms."

"Holy shit," I choked out as I retracted my swords and crumpled into Abaddon. "Every vision she saw was a thought in my mind. How? How did I do that?"

The Demon, who I loved, held me tight and rested his chin on my head. "I have no fucking clue," he admitted with a shaky laugh. "That's a power I've not seen before."

"It was like a freaking hologram," Cher said as she marched back over now that it was relatively safe I wasn't going to incinerate my friends. She pulled wine coolers from her bag and handed them out. "You've got some powerful mojo, girlie."

"Is this normal?" I asked. My voice was pitched about an octave too high. While I was cognizant that very little in my life was normal anymore, this new wrinkle might be a problem. If every stinking thought I had, became a three-dimensional image, I was screwed.

"Define normal," Sushi said with a chuckle as she accepted the libation and downed it. "I knew a tealeaf reader back in the day...a few thousand years ago. He could do the same thing."

"Did others see his every thought?" I asked, running my hands through my hair in frustration. Life had gone from barely manageable to a living nightmare. The thoughts I had about Abaddon alone made me want to go into hiding.

"No," she replied. "He controlled it."

"How?"

She shrugged and put the empty bottle back in Cher's purse. "I don't know."

"You talking about Atlas?" Cher questioned.

Sushi was surprised. "I am. Did you know him?"

"Banged him," Cher said with a laugh. "Great guy. Big dick."

"TMI," I said flatly. "Do you have any idea how he controlled showing his every waking thought?"

My Angel agent grinned. "As a matter of fact, I do."

I grabbed the woman and swung her around like a doll. She squealed and slapped at me.

Setting her back on her feet, I kissed her left cheek and then her right. Twice. "Tell me."

"Easy as pie," she assured me. "Atlas, God rest his big-peckered soul, used to just put a boulder in front of the door."

I scrunched my nose and wanted to take back the kisses. "Literally. A boulder?"

She giggled. "Metaphorically. Think of your mind as a warehouse filled with a bunch of junk."

"Fairly accurate," I commented.

Abaddon laughed. It was a rare sound coming from him and made me feel lighter.

Cher continued. "When you want people to tour the warehouse, open the big metal doors. When you want to keep your thoughts private, slam that bastard shut."

"Okay," I said, thinking nothing the Immortals did was this easy. There had to be a catch. I was about to find out. "I'm going to close my eyes and think of something with the door... umm open."

"Make sure it's something absurd. Not easily guessed," Sushi suggested.

"Good thinking," I replied. I closed my eyes and went with the first and most horrifying thing that came to mind. If the object in my mind were projected, there would be screams.

I pretended to open the warehouse doors and let my mind wander back to earlier this evening.

"Shit," I grumbled and I stood up. "This is getting ridiculous."

I refused to look up and see the underside of their balls. Marching over to the tree where they were perched, I looked straight ahead and spoke in my outdoor voice. Sadly, I faltered and glanced up. Their wrinkled testicles swayed in the breeze. I seriously wished mind bleach was a real thing. "Corny, what the hell do you think you're doing?"

"It's thrilling!" he shouted. "I had no clue that you lived in a nudist colony. It's my dream come true!"

"Jesus Herman Christ! NO," Cher shouted with a peal of laughter.

"Of all the visuals, that's what you picked?" Sushi shrieked.

"I need to gouge my eyes out," Abaddon muttered.

"You guys see it?" I asked with a wide grin.

"Unfortunately, yes," Abaddon replied.

"What is it?" I questioned with my eyes still closed and the icky visual still front and center.

"For the love of everything gas inducing," Cher choked out still laughing. "I see Uncle Joe and Corny's meat clackers. The old naked geezers are sitting in a damned tree. Their nuts a bouncing in the dang breeze."

"Bingo," I said, opening my eyes and looking around. Nothing was there. No Corny. No Uncle Joe and no balls. "I think I have to close my eyes to make it happen."

Abaddon sighed and shook his handsome head. "While I'm a bit terrified to suggest it, why don't you try again but close the warehouse doors first."

"On it," I said, closing my eyes. Without thinking about it too hard, in my mind, I pretended to slam the big metal door shut. The sound I imagined was satisfying and loud. This time I relived my horrible audition where I mistakenly thought I could fly. I winced as the humiliating memory came back...

The waiting room was bright green. I'd dressed in colorful sweats because I'd been told the final callback would be athletic. Since I didn't own colorful sweats, I'd made a quick run to the mall. Looking ridiculous was clearly part of the plan. I'd tried to get out of the final callback six times, but no go. My gut told me that I should bail. While my excuses had been pathetic, I hadn't grown big enough actress balls to stand up for myself yet.

I'd rolled my eyes hard when my agent at the time had informed me of the colorful sweats requirement... and that she'd drop me as a client if I bagged on the final round. I'd already "jumped funny" for the casting people and producers for over an hour in front of a green screen just the week before, pulling muscles I didn't know I had. I'd had to get a massage after that hot mess.

Yet, here I was... at the final callback. I'd almost stayed back in the waiting room, but I was not a quitter.

About ten network execs and three casting people sat in chairs drinking coffee and looking rabidly excited. It made my stomach hurt. I waved. They waved back. My competition, who I'd named Obnoxious Girl with Dumbass Pigtails, did a somersault, landed at their feet and saluted them. They laughed with delight.

Shit. Why didn't I think of that? Maybe because it was stupid? I was very aware that Obnoxious Girl with Dumbass Pigtails wasn't a very nice name for me to have secretly given her, but she'd not so secretly been calling me Vampire Girl throughout the seven callbacks we'd been through together. I suppose she thought that would psyche me out. She was wrong. I'd developed seriously thick skin during the years I'd logged in the biz. Being the Vampire Girl had bought me a house and a car. Obnoxious Girl with Dumbass Pigtails could kiss my ass.

The wrinkle was that there was a third person in the running who I'd never seen. He was a quiet guy with a friendly smile.

"Hey there! Hi there! Ho there, kids!" the director shouted at Obnoxious Girl with Dumbass Pigtails, Quiet Guy and me as he entered the audition space.

"Hey there! Hi there! Ho there to you too!" my competition shouted in her outdoor voice.

Dammit. Her sweats were more colorful than mine. My need to win fired up inside me. The fact that the job would put me into traction didn't matter.

"Hey doodley-do there! Hi woodley-woo there! Ho—not the bad kind—there to you too!" I screamed at the top of my lungs.

I wanted to die, but the attention was on me now. Winning. Although, everyone looked confused. I realized I probably shouldn't have made a reference to a hooker since this was a children's program.

"Hi everyone," Quiet Guy said politely.

The producers nodded, seemingly impressed that he could speak at a socially acceptable volume. I made a mental note to tone it down.

"Okay, kiddos," the director, who called himself Papa, announced. "We want to see if you can fly!"

I squinted at him. Papa was missing a few screws if he thought anyone could actually fly. "Literally?"

"You betcha," he shouted with a spastic thumbs up.

"Awesome!" Obnoxious Girl with Dumbass Pigtails yelled, doing an aerial cartwheel.

The crowd went nuts. I was no longer winning.

There was no way I could do an aerial without breaking my neck. However, I was thirty to forty percent sure I could do a diving front roll. The odds weren't the best, but if I did the dive in front of the camera filming us, it would look like I was flying.

"Who wants to go next?" Papa shouted.

"I will," Quiet Guy said with a shy smile.

"Have at it," Papa screamed, jumping up and down.

Papa was alarming. I hoped he wasn't the main director of the show. The urge to throat punch him was strong.

Quiet Guy walked to the center of the room and put his arms out in front of him. He slowly rocked back and forth as he appeared to be looking down at the world from the sky. "Such a lovely place," he said with an adorable grin. "The colors make my heart sing. And look! I can see my house. I feel like I'm a big airplane. It's amazing! Would you like to fly with me?" he asked the camera. "Great! Let's fly together."

I tried to gauge which flying the producers liked better. It was difficult to tell. They clapped just as loudly for Quiet Guy as they did for Obnoxious Girl with Dumbass Pigtails. Personally, I liked Quiet Guy's gentle style, but decided to go with the dive roll.

Big mistake. Huge. One of the hugest I'd ever made.

"You ready for your turn, Cecily?" Papa asked, bouncing up and down.

Watching a bald dude in his sixties called Papa bounce like a ball was scary.

"I am," I said at a volume that was about halfway between Quiet Guy and Obnoxious Girl with Dumbass Pigtails. "Every-one, stand back. I'm about to fly!"

Obnoxious Girl with Dumbass Pigtails glared at me. Quiet Guy gave me an encouraging thumbs up and a sweet smile. The producers were on the edge of their seats. My confidence soared.

Taking a running start, I dove as I passed the camera. The cheers were music to my ears. As I went for the forward roll, it didn't quite go as planned. Instead of a roll, I face planted. Hard.

"I'm fine," I shouted, swiping away the sweat from my face that I didn't realize was blood. I was pretty sure I heard screams, but my ears were ringing. I ignored them. "Let me try that again!"

I wasn't certain, but I thought I heard Papa yell, NO. The ear ringing was loud. I spit out the hard gum in my mouth that I'd forgotten I was chewing and went back to my starting point. The producers were on their feet. I took that as a great sign.

It wasn't.

As I ran toward the camera, I realized that the gum I'd spit out were my teeth. Needless to say, that threw me for a loop. But I kept going. The show must always go on, even if you're bleeding and toothless. I misjudged the camera—probably due to the blood from my mouth that had spread to my eyes—and hit it as I dove. The sharp edge caught my forehead, and it felt like I'd been slashed with a knife.

However, this time I did finish with a very nice forward roll.

Then I passed out. The last thing I recalled before I was out like a light, was Papa crying. Maybe he wasn't all that bad.

I opened my eyes. Cher, Sushi and Abaddon were quietly waiting.

"You didn't see that?" I asked, waiting for them to burst into laughter.

"Didn't see a thing." Cher clapped me on the shoulder. "Good work!"

"One thing accomplished. Many more to go," I patted my beautiful gown to make sure my meltdown hadn't singed holes in the fabric. Amazingly, it was good as new. Magic was bizarrely unexplainable. "As much as it would delight me to give you all indigestion with my warped imagination, we need to go the palace and face Lilith's Demons."

"Your Demons," Abaddon corrected me.

I looked at him for a long beat. "I hope so."

He winked. "I know so."

CHAPTER NINE

A CASTLE OF PURE GOLD STOOD HIGH AND MAJESTIC AS IF IT had come straight from the pages of a fairytale...on crack. Sparkling pointed towers reached into the inky sky and shimmered in the red sunlight. We stood on steps encrusted with jewels—diamonds, rubies, emeralds and sapphires. I'd bet my career that they were real. Blood-red rose vines snaked up the sky-high palace walls seemingly holding the place together. Red poppies and hibiscus dominated the surrounding landscape. The moat, if you could call it that, was more like a turbulent river filled with fangy, slimy green mini-monsters that surrounded the massive and ornate structure.

There was no way to tell what time it was here. At home it was the middle of the night. Here? With the dark purple sky and the blazing sun, I didn't have a clue.

After seeing the lovely safehouse that Lilith had built, I couldn't imagine her living in the monstrosity I stood in front of. I sure as hell never wanted to live here. I much preferred my quaint little Craftsman in Venice Beach.

"It's showtime, folks," I whispered as the butterflies in my stomach came back with a vengeance.

I didn't look to Abaddon to tell me how to proceed. I didn't ask Ophelia to have my back. I had no intention of asking my agent to represent me on this job. And I wasn't going to command Sushi to take out any naysayers with a bang. Pun intended.

I was going with my gut. I was in charge. If the Demons didn't believe it, there was no way I would earn their trust. We faced the palace, but I was very aware we were not alone. Slowly turning around, I let my gaze sweep over the valley below.

I didn't have to worry about calling *my* people. They were already here.

The sea of stunning male and female Demons appeared endless. Thousands of them had gathered on the other side of the moat. The expressions on the faces I could see were ones of wariness and sorrow.

"Is it true that the Goddess Lilith has perished?" a booming voice from the crowd bellowed.

The acoustics in the Darkness were outstanding. The man's voice echoed like we were in a canyon. I glanced around for speakers or a mic, but there was nothing.

I stepped forward and addressed the masses. "It's true."

The wails and screams of the Demons tore at my heart. I'd felt the very same way when I'd held her dead body in my arms.

I kept going and let my voice boom and carry across the

valley. "The Goddess Lilith is dead. The human Lilith remains."

The crowd went silent. I wasn't sure if that was good or bad, but I definitely had their attention.

"I'm Cecily Bloom. Daughter of Lilith."

"Lies. Heresy," a female in the front hissed. "We would have known. She would have told us. You shall be put to death."

My eyes narrowed to slits, and the woman backed away. I realized with an almost inaudible gasp that I was glowing. Whatever. That was the least of my worries at the moment. The asshole in the front just called for my death. I was getting really sick and tired of people wanting to kill me.

"Would you have known?" I demanded. She couldn't look at me. "WOULD YOU HAVE?"

"If it's true then you killed the Goddess," another shouted. "You wanted her power and riches. You murdered her for it."

I rolled my eyes and electrocuted the jerk. I needed to say my piece without worrying if someone would charge across the bridge and try to lop my head off. I didn't think. I just went with my gut. Waving my hands, I froze every single Demon in front of me. I was shocked it worked. So were they. Sadly, it didn't work on their mouths. The shouts and insults were loud, plentiful and profane. I hoped that I hadn't inadvertently frozen Abaddon, Ophelia, Cher and Sushi, but I couldn't look back. My future was in front of me... even though I didn't really want it. Being in charge of a bunch of dicks wasn't my idea of a good time.

"Here's the deal," I snapped. "I love my mother. She loves

me. She kept both me and all of you in the dark my entire
life until recently. It was for my safety and, ultimately,
yours. So... you're stuck with me."

"What qualifications do you have?" a man yelled out
from the back somewhere.

The short answer was none, but I didn't think that
would go over very well. The phrase the truth will set you
free came to mind... It was also a whole lot easier to
remember the truth than lies. However, it could also end in
bloodshed—mine.

Facts. I would go with the undisputable facts.

"I'm a direct bloodline of Lilith. Her wish is that I take
her place as your goddess. It's my birthright to do so," I said
as my mind raced for something impressive. Shit. Improv
wasn't my thing. Didn't matter. I was here to do the fuck
out of it. If I'd been even an iota aware of the word salad I
was about to vomit up, I would have cut my losses and run.

Hindsight is twenty-twenty.

"I've singlehandedly ended the existence of quite a few
flaming assholes." The crowd looked confused. Crap.
"Umm... I went after the Shitty Whore and came very close
to taking her out. Which I'm aware is a big no-no, but she
had killed my mother."

"Wait," a gorgeous female at the end of the bridge
shouted. "What is a flaming asshole, and who's a shitty
whore?"

"You're a shitty whore," another female next to her
snarled.

I electrocuted the bitchy one. The other gal asked a good
question. Ignoring that the rude one was on fire, I addressed

the more polite of the two Demons, though polite might be a stretch. At least, she wasn't being nasty.

"A flaming asshole is one who's loyal to Pandora. Shitty Whore is what I call Pandora."

The crowd went from hostile to... well, I wasn't sure what to call it. They started laughing, and they couldn't stop. I was pretty sure they were laughing at me and not with me, but it was better than having my life threatened. I did feel kind of bad that Bitchy Demon was consumed in flames. Wiggling my fingers, I doused the fire. Of course, I drenched her so she wasn't quite so stunning.

"More," the Demons yelled in unison. "More. More!"

I stole a quick glance over my shoulder at Abaddon. It wasn't clear if his expression was one of mortification or if he needed to go to the bathroom. I decided not to analyze it.

Sucking in a deep breath, I went for it. "I'm an actress by trade. I starred in a show called *Camp Bite* for years."

"I loved *Camp Bite*," someone cried out.

"Brilliant," another shouted.

The murmurs of appreciation for the silly show I'd spent my childhood doing gave me more confidence. Probably misguided, but confidence nonetheless.

"I've done a number of crappy movies of the week and a few good ones. I've been fired from a sitcom for not having a big enough ass, and in my twenties, I tried to fly at an audition for a kid's TV show. I knocked out a few teeth and have a couple of scars to prove it. It was recorded. It's probably on the internet if you search it." My insanity wasn't bubbling below the surface. It was out and proud. I couldn't believe what I'd just shared, but it seemed to be going over well. Maybe I wasn't as bad at improv as I'd thought.

The Demons were now shrieking with laughter. So, what did I do? I kept going.

"I've done a few informercials and more national commercials than you could shake a stick at. The only jobs I ever passed on were those for sexually transmitted diseases, anything to do with the vagina and ones where they wanted me to go topless."

Again, with the riotous cackling.

It felt great. I'd never performed for such a big audience. However, this wasn't a comedy show. It was not fiction. It was real and this wasn't working for me. Although, I was still unclear on what the Goddess of the Darkness did on a day-to-day basis, I knew it wasn't stand-up comedy.

Holding my hands up, I quieted the crowd. If I was going to do the fuck out of it, I needed to be sincere. I couldn't force the Demons to follow me. Heck, I didn't want to have to keep looking over my shoulder all the time. If they didn't want to give me a shot, it was on them.

"Here's the truth. I'm not sure I want the job. Lilith insists that it's mine because I'm her daughter. I think she's a bit insane."

"All the best ones are," a busty red headed Demon assured me.

I gave her a smile. "I don't know what I'm doing. I don't know what you expect. But I promise you this. I'll be fair and compassionate. Murder isn't my strong point, but if it's me or the bad guy... or you or the bad guy, I'll pick you and me, and I'll kick ass."

I began to pace back and forth. I thought better when I moved. Speaking from my heart was what my gut told me to do. I refused to check in with my posse. This was my episode, and I was playing it out until the end with no commercial breaks.

"A few weeks ago," I continued. "I was just a forty-year-old actress trying to make a comeback in Hollywood. Now? I'm a whole lot more. My power's immense—scared the heck out of me at first. The Grim Reaper did a spell to help me control it. That's good for all of us, especially the land masses on Earth."

The Demons listened intently, and their eyes followed me back and forth like I was the ball in a tennis match. It felt wrong to have them immobile. Fixing it could be a mistake, but if they wanted to try and take me out, I wished them luck. I was seriously hard to kill.

"I'm going to unfreeze you. If you come at me, it will be the last thing you do." I slashed my hands through the air and set them free. Crossing my fingers that I hadn't FUBARed, I kept going. "You have a choice that I will respect no matter what you decide to do. If you want to stay with me, I would be honored. If you don't... then you're on your own. I'd suggest you not give your allegiance to the Shitty Whore. My mission is to put the bitch back in her box and leave her there for a good long while. Fair warning, if you side with the skank, you might go down with her. I'm done with her crap, and I'm ending it."

"You had me at Shitty Whore," the Demon who asked for clarification earlier called out. She gave me a thumbs up.

A sophisticated gentleman stepped forward. "I'm

inclined to pledge my fealty to you, but something feels missing."

I stared at him. If he wanted me to beg, he'd be waiting a very long time.

A blonde bombshell walked to the mouth of the bridge and looked me up and down. Her face was pinched with distrust. "Prove that you didn't take the life of our Goddess. I think you're a lying viper. You came here with an Angel and a Succubus, thinking you're the bigshot. You're nothing." Her tone was harsh, her glare venomous, and her face red with ire.

The Demons collectively gasped, but none made a move to defend me.

Two could play her game. I leveled her with a stare that epitomized the phrase, 'If looks could kill, she'd be dead.' After a full minute of silent stare-off she lowered her gaze.

"You," I snapped, pointing at her. "Name?"

"Zada," she replied.

Without looking back, I made a request. "Cher, please write that name down. I love lists. Especially naughty and nice lists."

Zada hissed, but the others chuckled. I'd learned quickly that Demons respected violence and bad behavior. I wasn't a real violent gal, but I could give an outstanding verbal lashing. Joan Crawford had nothing on me.

"Got it," Cher said.

I made a decision. It had become increasingly obvious that very little happened in the Immortal world that wasn't for a reason. I could project visions. If they wanted proof, they would have proof. "Abaddon. Ophelia. Please flank me.

I have to close my eyes to do this, and I don't trust my audience."

The crowd gasped in indignation as my love and my friend moved in to protect me.

My eye roll was enormous. "Give me a break," I shouted. "Would you trust you if you were me?"

No one could refute it.

Closing my eyes, I made sure the warehouse door was wide open. I didn't want to relive what I'd already witnessed, but fair was fair. I'd promised them that. Pulling up the memory was hard, but nothing worthwhile was easy.

The vicious Goddess waved her hand. In a flash of lightning and a crash of thunder, at least fifty flaming assholes appeared. The smile on her lips was psychotic. "Kill Cecily Bloom!"

Lilith, Dagon, Abaddon and I fought the army of evil with all we had... and we had a lot. My mother was a freaking killing machine. She was balletic, precise and terrifying. For the most part, the flaming assholes avoided her. They knew who she was and that ending her was forbidden. Dagon was no slouch, but Abaddon fought like a crazed animal.

Blow by blow. Electrocution by electrocution. It was a bloody mess. I'd lost part of my left hand but was still able to grip my sword.

Pandora stood back and watched. Her cowardice was astounding. I might die, but she was going down.

The enemy went from fifty down to twelve quickly. However, the last dozen were determined.

"Cecily, leave," Lilith yelled over the ruckus. "Now."

I wanted to obey her. I really did, but I couldn't. This was my battle. I needed to fight it. "Not until she's back in her box," I shouted.

Everything that came next happened fast, but I would replay it in slow motion for the rest of my days. Pandora began to lob explosive fireballs. I screamed in agony when one hit my leg. I refused to look down to see if my leg was still there. The searing pain made me come close to throwing up. Moving away from the sizzling fire, I realized that even though I had third-degree burns or worse, I could still stand. I kept my eyes on Pandora's hands while trying to defend myself from her Demons.

Abaddon was at my side immediately. In the millisecond it took for me to acknowledge him, I saw a flaming asshole come up behind him wielding a fiery sword.

"Duck," I shouted at the love of my life.

Abaddon escaped being beheaded, but Pandora saw her opening. The ball of fire she hurled at me was massive, deadly and had my name all over it. I tried to dodge it, but my leg hindered my escape. The aggressive push from my right side sent me flying into Abaddon. The explosion was brutal. The building creaked on its foundation.

"What have you done?" Dagon roared in a voice so furious, I felt lightheaded.

"It's not my fault," Pandora shrieked, having a panic attack.

The Goddess pulled on her hair and ran her sharp nails down her arms, leaving behind trails of oozing blood. I didn't understand what was happening... until I did.

Lilith lay collapsed on the floor where I had been only moments ago. Her beautiful body was broken and battered. The light was gone. Her life was gone. She bled profusely from her mouth and her chest wasn't moving.

The realization was hard to comprehend. It didn't make any sense, but the proof was in front of me. She died for me. My mother had brought me into this world, and now she'd sacrificed herself to keep me in it. This was all wrong.

I'd never seen red in my life. I'd heard about it but had never experienced it until now. My body heated up like a roaring furnace. My tongue felt like steaming hot sandpaper, and my vision blurred with hatred. With a scream of rage so raw I was sure my throat was bleeding, I slashed my hands through the air. The last twelve flaming assholes combusted into flames while screaming in agony. The six who had been stunned by the lipsticks exploded as well. Good riddance to horrible rubbish. I smiled. It didn't reach my eyes.

"Eighteen down," I hissed at Pandora. "One to go. Get ready to die, shitty whore."

I ran at her with inhuman speed in a fit of all-consuming anger. My purple fire swords were aimed at her neck. She owed me her life, and I would exact the payment.

I'd never told my mother I loved her. I'd never hugged her. Now I'd never get the chance.

As I swung my swords with all my might, Pandora disappeared in a blast of black glitter. I fell to the ground from the intensity of my blows that hadn't even touched her. I stared in shock at the ground where she'd stood only moments earlier.

"No, no, no," I cried out.

Tears rolled down my cheeks as I opened my eyes. Abaddon put his hand on my shoulder to comfort me. I smiled and gave his hand a squeeze. "I've got this," I whispered.

"I know you do," he said with love and pride in his eyes. "A little unconventional, but classic Cecily."

"That's Bitch Goddess Cecily to you," I said with a grin.

I walked to the middle of the bridge. Alone. My eyes roved over the Demons who had just witnessed the death of their beloved Goddess. It wasn't an easy watch. The tears flowed freely, and their eyes were glued to me.

It started with one lone Demon deep in the crowd. The clap sounded like a shot in the night. It startled me. Another Demon joined, then another... then another. Soon, thousands of Demons were applauding. The sound echoed and made it seem like hundreds of thousands were participating. It was overwhelming and humbling.

"All hail the Goddess Cecily!" the sophisticated man bellowed, bowing in respect.

En masse they followed his lead. A bizarre feeling of completion washed over me. A month ago, if someone had told me how the show of my life would play out, I would have canceled the entire production. Today was a different story. I still wasn't a hundred percent sure I could cut it as the Goddess of the Darkness, but I was going to open my mind to change and give it my best. I would keep my promise of being fair and compassionate. And I would reach my goal of putting Pandora back in her box. My mother deserved it. My people deserved it. I deserved it.

Raising my hands into the air, I produced both purple fire swords. The Demons went silent then dropped to their knees. You could have heard a pin drop into a bed of soft soil.

I smiled at my people. "I am Bitch Goddess Cecily." My

gaze swept the crowd. "Your Bitch Goddess Cecily, and I'd suggest you remember that."

The cheering was wild. The chants of Bitch Goddess Cecily made me laugh. I'd signed the life-long contract, and it was ironclad. The script for my new role wasn't yet written. It was a work in progress.

After a few hours of greeting my people, we left with a promise to return soon. The plot of the next episode of the show was finding the Shitty Whore and dealing with her. With the full support of the Demons under my reign, I felt stronger and more confident.

It was time to get the party started.

CHAPTER TEN

THE TRIP BACK HOME HAD BEEN A LOT LESS BUMPY THAN THE trip into the Darkness. We'd accomplished our goals, but now there was another wrinkle.

"What language is that?" I asked, squinting at the squiggles on the weathered and yellowed pages of the thick book. It was ancient and leatherbound. It looked strangely out of place on my coffee table, but the good thing was that we had it. It would be even better if we could read it.

"A dead language," Cher muttered, trying to make sense of it.

Corny, Moon and Irma had found the book and absconded with it. Pandora's people had fought hard but hadn't won. The Succubi army, led by Fifi, had only banged fifty flaming assholes into dust. Fifi wasn't one of the bangers. The others who posed an issue were thoroughly maimed. Fifi was front and center on the maiming part. Many grenades had been detonated. If I thought about the visuals, my stomach roiled.

Sushi and Fifi had taken her army back to Vegas to put the *bangers* into a sex rehab program. My Succubus self-appointed bodyguard promised to return quickly.

I'd thanked Sushi profusely and told her I owed her a favor. I hoped that didn't come back to bite me in the ass, but it was the right thing to do. Abaddon didn't appear too pleased with my offer to the Queen of the Succubi but didn't comment.

Corny was missing an arm. Irma was minus a leg. Moon was all in one piece. Cher had healed the giddy Demons, and Abaddon had called both Candy Vargo and Lilith to get them up to speed.

"It was thrilling!" Corny gushed as I handed him one of my old bathrobes. He was as naked as the day he was born. He didn't want to be encumbered by clothing on his mission. Apparently, his flapping nuts had provided a moment of confusion to Pandora's warriors during my crews' escape. The Succubi, not ones to miss an opportunity, had taken the opening and went to town. "The henchmen were in the grand ballroom playing Bingo when we arrived. We had no problem sneaking into the library. It was the exit that was a little more complicated."

"The Tome of Dark Magic was in the same spot as all those centuries ago," Moon chimed in. "But the kicker was it was under enchanted glass."

"Which posed a snag," Corny explained. "Irma tried beating the shit out of it with an axe."

"Didn't work," Irma volunteered. "I even morphed into my mouse form to see if that would freak it out."

"No luck," Moon added. "However, Irma's mouse made Corny pee himself."

"Ohhh yes!" Corny said, not even remotely embarrassed. "I used the accident to spray the glass with my healthy golden stream. I had the brilliant idea that urine might dissolve the spell."

"Are you brain damaged?" Cher asked him.

"Define brain damaged," Corny replied, confused.

"Anyhoo," Irma quickly chimed in before the conversation could go farther south than it already had. "Moon was the gal who came through!"

"I'm kind of scared to ask, but how did Moon come through?" I inquired.

Moon Sunny Swartz smirked like a fool and rotated her hips. My mouth fell open. Cher cackled. Ophelia gagged, and Abaddon groaned.

"No way," I said, unsure whether to laugh or scream. "You humped it?"

"Humped that sucker until it begged for mercy," Moon announced, pumping her fists over her head.

"It was wonderous and slightly disgusting," Corny confirmed, patting Moon on the back. "Our girl gyrated, slamdogged and hunka-chunked that enchantment into dust."

"I puked a little in my mouth," Irma admitted. "But it worked. Moon's cooch is a weapon!"

Moon took a bow. She got a weak round of applause. "Taking one for the team is what I do. In the future, I'd be delighted to hump all of our problems away."

"Umm… thank you," I told her. "I seriously hope that won't be necessary."

"Word," Ophelia muttered.

Moon turned to Cher. "Should I put humping down on my resume under special skills?"

"Absolutely not," Cher said in a brook no bullshit tone.

Moon gave her a thumbs up and a lewd hip thrust.

"It was truly fucking crazy," Irma said with a wide grin. "Haven't had so much fun since I got cast in the off-off-off Broadway Viagra musical—*Have Dick Will Travel.*"

"Do *not* put that on your resume, either," Cher told her.

Irma laughed and dug into the pile of pizzas that Uncle Joe had somehow ordered.

"As I said earlier, the escape was a bit of a hassle," Corny went on.

"Understatement," Irma said with a mouthful of pizza. "However, those freaking Succubi are insane."

Moon nodded her head in awed agreement. "And I thought my hoohaw was a weapon."

"Okay," I said, cutting them off before they went into the specifics of the Succubi banging the enemy to death. My imagination was bad enough. The detailed graphics were something I didn't need to know. Ever. "Everyone eat, please."

My dear and dead relative zipped around the room making sure everyone had refreshment.

"How did you make this happen?" I asked him, digging into the sausage and pepperoni.

Uncle Joe giggled. "I texted the order and used your

credit card. I left explicit instructions to leave the pies on the porch since I'm dead."

"Umm… did you actually tell them you're dead?" I asked, almost choking.

"Whoopsiedoodle," Joe said, smacking himself on the forehead. "While the truth is I am *dead*, I wrote that I was *deaf*. Used a little typo to my advantage. I so hate to lie, but figured they'd think it was a prank call if I told the truth."

"Excellent thinking, Joe!" Corny exclaimed.

"Thank you, friend," Uncle Joe replied with a wink and a shimmy.

I scrunched my nose and looked away. It looked like something might be developing between Corny and my uncle. I wasn't sure how that would work since Joe was deceased and all, but it wasn't my business… thankfully.

Abaddon studied the pages. His expression was perplexed. "I've not seen this script before."

"Me neither," Cher said, scratching her head. "And I thought I'd seen them all."

"I'd suggest calling Lilith in," he said. "There's a fine chance that the language was written for the goddesses only."

"Shouldn't I be able to read it then?" I asked, getting up and walking back over to the book.

Abaddon shrugged. "I could be wrong. Give it another try."

I sat down on the floor next to the book and lightly ran my fingers over the paper. "How do we know we're on the right page?"

"You opened the book. Correct?" Abaddon asked.

I nodded.

"Then you're on the right page," he assured me.

Getting used to the cryptic was going to take some time. I just hoped he was right.

The squiggles were curved and surrounded by random numbers of dots. It was unclear if it was to be read from right to left, left to right or up and down. The Higher Power was a turd. The harder I stared, the more the symbols blurred. I didn't give up. I wasn't a quitter.

"Not working," I muttered.

"Should I hump it?" Moon asked.

I didn't answer her, but Ophelia did with a left hook.

"Guess that's a no," Moon said, nursing her cheek.

As I continued to stare, the dots began to rise off the paper. A tingle of excitement shot through me. I wiggled my fingers and coaxed the dots further from the page. They appeared to obey as they began to reformulate into words. I gasped, observing the ancient message as it began to take shape and become something I inherently recognized.

"Oh my God," I whispered. "I can see it."

"Speak it aloud," Abaddon insisted tightly.

"Taking notes," Cher said, pulling out an eyeliner pencil and grabbing an empty pizza box.

A chilly wind danced through my living room and diamond-like crystals appeared as the letters lined up.

I cleared my throat and read the words.

"The vessel breathes. The box is within. Find it. Open it. Hope will win."

The dots popped and dropped back onto the page as I

read the last word. The silence in the room was loud. I'd
read it but had no clue what it meant.

"Anybody?" I asked.

"Nope," Cher said.

"Let's break it down." Abaddon looked over Cher's
shoulder at the notes she had taken. "The vessel breathes
suggests that it's a living entity of some kind."

"A living box?" I asked.

"You know," Moon said. "Box could also mean vagina.
Vaginas are alive as long as they're connected. It's a possibility that we're searching for a sentient cooch."

"What the actual fuck?" Ophelia snapped as Moon dove
behind the couch to avoid another punch to the head.

"I'm going to stop you right there, Moon," I said,
pressing the bridge of my nose. "While I truly appreciate the
input, my gut tells me we're not looking for a vagina."

"Alrighty then." Abaddon scrubbed his hands over his
jaw to hide his expression of disbelief. "Moving on. The box
is within most likely means it's hidden inside something."

"Makes sense," I said.

"The rest is obvious," he stated. "We need to find it. Open
it and let the one thing Pandora hasn't let out of it win."

"Hope," I whispered.

Ophelia snapped her fingers. "Bingo, bitch!"

"We have the key." Closing the book, I stood up and
repeated what Lilith had told me. "The truth can shift. In
the Darkness, the seed of hope awaits. Behind every smile
lies a dark secret. What you see is rarely what you get. Some
bridges are meant to be burned. Embrace what is repugnant

to discover the beauty that lies beneath. Often the answer has been in front of you the entire time."

"The key doesn't seem to fit the lock," Cher commented. "It's a lot like trying to force a square peg into a round hole."

"I have to believe it fits…somehow," I replied. "We just haven't figured it out yet." I needed more help than my current crew could provide, which meant… "I need to take a trip."

"To?" Abaddon asked.

"The safehouse," I replied, extending my hand. "Come with me."

He smiled and took my hand firmly in his. "As you wish." Lifting my hand to his lips, he brushed a light kiss across my knuckles then pinned me with his dark gaze. "There's no place else I'd rather be."

My knees wobbled as the warmth of his breath on my skin made my insides dance with joy.

"That was hot," Ophelia said as Irma, Cher and Moon enthusiastically agreed.

"Do I hear wedding bells?" Uncle Joe asked with a delighted smile.

I giggled. "Umm… we're just dating at the moment. I'll let you know when and if that changes."

Abaddon's grin was sexy, naughty and filled with lustful promise. "I do believe you're supposed to embrace change," he said with a raised brow and twinkling eyes.

My knees went a little rubbery again, and I held on to him so I didn't hit the floor with an embarrassing thud. "So are you," I retorted.

"I'm all in," he replied smoothly. "Let me know when you are."

I wanted to kiss him so badly, I could taste it. However, if I kissed him, I knew I would never stop. Kissing was a gateway to banging, and banging my Demon for the first time in a roomful of people wasn't my style.

"Soon," I promised with a look that made him gulp. "Very soon."

CHAPTER ELEVEN

At least thirty armed Demons patrolled the property around the safehouse. When we arrived in a gust of glittering black and silver dust, they bowed to me in respect. I'd thanked them and took some time to introduce myself to each of them. The group was comprised of both men and women. Abaddon had assured me that they were some of the highest skilled and deadliest warriors we had. That sat very right with me. My family was my world. Keeping them safe was a top priority.

The interior of the safehouse was perfect with my mom and dad in it. Man-mom had been delightedly shocked that it was Lilith who'd collected his art over the years. Both of them were so happy and at peace. They'd decided to make the lovely cottage their permanent home. I'd miss Man-mom living next door with Sean, but the thought of visiting my parents, finally together, at the safehouse filled me with joy.

Sean fit right in as well. He sat at the kitchen table with his laptop open. From what I could tell, he'd written two more episodes of *Ass The World Turns*, including our new and slightly scary cast members. My brother was the bomb and the fastest writer I knew.

Stella and Jonny had made themselves at home. They were playing board games in the living room, both of them cheating.

"I'm so proud of you, Cecily," Lilith said after I'd given her a play by play of claiming my place as the Bitch Goddess Cecily. Her eyes had gone wide a few times during the recounting, but I'd soldiered on.

It was a new chapter in the Demon story and if I was going to do the fuck out of it, I had to do it my way. Sticking my foot in my mouth and metaphorically pulling it out of my ass was going to happen from time to time. Hopefully, not all of the time.

We'd have to wait and see.

"What about the Tome of Dark Magic?" Lilith inquired. "Did you bring it?"

I shook my head. "No. But I was able to read it."

Her brows shot up as she laughed. "Of course, you were. You, my daughter, are far more powerful than anyone knows. Even me. Remember, with great power comes even greater responsibility."

"That makes me a little gassy, mom," I admitted.

"You'll get used to it," she promised. "Tell me what you found."

Abaddon had brought the pizza box that had the words scribbled on it with us just in case I forgot the exact wording. He hadn't needed to worry. I might be a newbie goddess, but I was a seasoned pro when it came to memorizing lines. Acting my whole life had guaranteed it.

"The vessel breathes. The box is within. Find it. Open it. Hope will win," I recited.

Lilith was perplexed. Her forehead wrinkled in thought as she mulled over what I'd said. That wasn't a great sign. I was hoping she'd know what it meant.

"The key you gave me doesn't quite fit either," I said, feeling a little panicky.

The book was supposed to solve our problem. It seemed it was just creating more. Lilith took the pizza box from Abaddon and studied it. I hoped to the Darkness and back that something would ring a bell for her. If not, we were screwed.

Sean ambled over and offered me a gummy. I passed.

"Say the words again," he instructed.

"The vessel breathes. The box is within. Find it. Open it. The hope will win," I repeated.

"Now, the key," he requested.

I shared it. "The truth can shift. In the Darkness, the seed of hope awaits. Behind every smile lies a dark secret. What you see is rarely what you get. Some bridges are meant to be burned. Embrace what is repugnant to discover the beauty that lies beneath. Often the answer has been in front of you the entire time."

He sat down on the chair, leaned back and grinned. "Seems kind of obvious to me. Slightly muddy plotline, but the meat is all there."

All eyes in the room shot to my brother. He wasn't a

Demon. He wasn't Immortal. But I was hoping with everything I was made of, we were about to get schooled by my human sibling.

"Who wrote it?" he asked.

"The Higher Power," I replied. "Why?"

Sean chuckled. "He'd make a good poet—very abstract."

I refrained from going over the fact that the Higher Power wasn't a he or she. It just was. It still confused me and probably always would. "Tell me how you would interpret it, please."

"The box is Pandora," he stated. "Pandora is the box. Lilith said in the beginning she was good. Now, she's not. My guess is that the evil has been seeping out of her for millions of years. Which, by the way, has to suck. That Higher Power dude has one warped sense of humor. The key tells you that hope still lives inside her. That's the only thing that hasn't escaped."

"Holy shit," Abaddon muttered, staring at Sean in shock.

Both Stella and Jonny were speechless. Their mouths hung open. Lilith gazed at Sean in amazement. Man-mom chuckled, walked over to his son and gave him a bear hug.

I was surprised, even though I shouldn't have been. Sean Bloom was like no one else in the Universe.

"I believe he's correct," Lilith said, joining Man-mom in hugging Sean. "I feel it in my gut. Cecily?"

I nodded. "Yep. Sean for the win. A huge, enormous, mammoth, giant, immense, gargantuan win."

Sean rolled his eyes. "What are you? A freaking thesaurus?"

"Yes," I said, bowing to my brother. "I'm Bitch Goddess

Cecily, the walking thesaurus and sister to the smartest Devil's Lettuce connoisseur in the history of mankind."

"I'm putting that on a t-shirt," Sean warned me. "And I'm wearing it every day."

I laughed. "Now we just have to find Pandora."

"And do what with her?" Stella asked. "I mean if she's the box, how do you put her inside herself?"

She'd made an excellent point. "I have no idea. I'll figure out the next scene while we look for her."

"Finding her won't be easy," Lilith said, concerned. "If Candy Vargo hasn't been able to do it, I'm not sure you'll have much more luck."

I flopped down on the couch, leaned forward and let my head rest in my hands. "Is everything in the Immortal world so freaking complicated? And is every situation life or death all the time?"

No one replied. That was my answer. I let Lilith's advice float in my brain—*The goal is peace. The obstacles will be many. Demons can be a violent species. However, they want to live in harmony like any other being. To help them accomplish that you must accept change as must they. You must seek support, focus on the goal and not the obstacles. Embrace your failures as much as you celebrate your wins. Most importantly, you must be as compassionate with yourself as you are with others and stay humble. Pride is the sin that destroys.*

"That's it," I shouted, making everyone jump.

"What's it?" Abaddon demanded.

I stood up and circled the living room. "What's the sin that destroys?"

"Pride," Lilith answered.

"Exactly," I said, getting more excited. "We might not be able to find Pandora, but if we rip away at her pride, I'd bet she'll find us."

"Draw her to you. Brilliant!" Jonny said, saluting me.

I saluted him right back.

"The question is, how?" Lilith said.

That was the part I hadn't figured out yet. "Well, she's vain. We know that."

"I say we insult the hell out of the Shitty Whore," Stella suggested. "Like *really* insult her. We could put up posters all over the Darkness with her face on them... BUT we draw mustaches, warts and boogers."

"Umm... not sure that's going far enough," I told her, trying not to laugh.

"What if we put it on the Demon Network?" Jonny suggested. "There's a fine chance she'll see that. The boogers will kill her."

"Demon Network?" Sean asked, intrigued.

Lilith chimed in. "Is a television network for Demons. It's accessed by a code on any enchanted computer."

"Like that one?" he asked, pointing to the glowing laptop Abaddon had given him.

"Yes," Lilith confirmed. "However, the line-up of shows —and I use the word show lightly—is appalling."

"It was created and run by Pandora," Abaddon told my brother. "She tends to broadcast torture, violence and lewd sex acts."

"She also broadcasts herself talking, or rather, threatening her people," Stella added with a snort of disgust. "All the time."

"Not sure posting crappy photoshopped pictures will bring her to us," I said, racking my brain for something far worse.

"I tend to agree with that," Lilith added. "Also, I'm unsure how we'd put anything up on the Demon Network anyway. I'm quite positive Pandora has the broadcast building locked down tight."

Sean turned and looked pointedly at Man-mom. Our dad blushed a deep red and ran his hands thorough his hair. "Do you have anything to add to the conversation, Bill?"

"It's been a long time," my dad admitted sheepishly.

I wasn't following the conversation. "Been a long time since what?"

"Shall I? Or shall you?" Sean asked with a shit-eating grin.

"I shall," Man-mom said, rubbing his hands together and sighing dramatically. "Well, umm…hmm. Not sure how to say it."

"Words would be good," I suggested, wondering what the heck was going on.

He chuckled. "When you were on *Camp Bites*, I had a job of sorts."

"You taught art," I reminded him.

"No, actually I didn't."

I looked at Sean. He was loving this. I was not.

"Okay, I'll bite. If you weren't teaching art, what were you doing?"

"CIA," he whispered.

I squinted at him in disbelief. "CIA? Like in the Central Intelligence Agency CIA?"

"Yes," he replied. "I'm a trained international hacker, for lack of a better way to put it. Got out when you kids hit high school. It became a little too dangerous for my liking."

A feather could have knocked me over. My attention snapped to Sean. "Why do you know this and I don't?"

"He talks in his sleep," Sean informed me. "I asked him about it, and he played dumb. So… I did what any devious son would do and recorded his sleep-talking. Got some really good incriminating shit. Let him listen to it, and the old man came clean. Easy peasy. Erased all of it after he admitted the truth. Can't have the feds up our asses. I have too many pot plants growing in the yard."

"Well, I'll be damned," I muttered. Was anything I knew about anything or anyone even remotely correct?

"We're all damned," Stella chimed in. "We're Demons."

"Thanks for that," I told her with an eye roll.

"Welcome," she replied.

"Sooooo," Sean continued. "My guess is that Man-mom can hack into the Demon Network if we want to go that way."

"Is that accurate?" I asked my dad.

Lilith seemed delighted with my dad's covert and probably unethical past. She wrapped her arms around him and kissed his cheek. "So sexy."

"It's accurate," Man-mom confirmed after kissing her back. "All I need is the password to get on the network, then I can access the dark web back channels to get to the broadcast signal."

I blinked rapidly. "Wow, that sounded totally professional."

Man-mom's grin verged on a preen.

"I have a password," Abaddon said. When I glanced askance at him, he added, "You need it if you want to offload misinformation to the right buyers."

Ah. In other words, he'd used it to feed a load of crap to some of Pandora's flaming assholes. My dad hadn't been the only one with a secret agent-type past.

I had questions, but those could wait. "If Man-mom is able to hack the signal, we need to televise something big to really draw Pandora out," I stated.

"If I come to the rescue twice, what do I get?" Sean inquired, crossing his arms over his chest with great satisfaction.

"What do you want?" I asked, a little wary. However, if he came up with a plan that could work, I'd give him whatever he wanted as long as it didn't put him in harm's way.

"A day at the airport. Me, you and Abaddon. We partake in a few gummies, lay on the hood of my car and watch the planes take off while reciting off the cuff poetry inspired by our buzz. Followed by lunch at my favorite diner."

Abaddon's brows raised in surprise. "I thought the reward would be monetary."

Sean grinned. "I'm not in it for the money. I much prefer meaningful experiences."

"While high," I added with a laugh. "Deal."

Sean glanced over at Abaddon. "And you, fine sir, who has the hots for my sister?"

Abaddon shook his head and groaned. "Deal."

"Excellent," Sean said. "Picture this. A sitcom on the Demon Network starring the Bitch Goddess Cecily of *Camp*

Bite fame. She's dealing with daily Demon life as a new Goddess and learning the ins and outs of the Darkness. She has a normal albeit not very smart human family and an incredibly shitty next-door neighbor. The neighbor causes all kinds of mischief but fails miserably and hilariously at every single turn. We can have her slip and fall in dog crap, have uncontrollable flatulence after she steals cookies from Cecily's house and eats them all in one sitting right before the HOA meeting that she's running—stuff like that. Absurd and stupid. We'll use all the crappy sitcom blunders and tropes—dumb dad versus uptight mom, awful catchphrases, we'll have a dinner scene where all the food looks amazing and no one eats, and all the characters have time-consuming jobs but never seem to work. You following?" he inquired with a sneaky little grin.

"Does the shitty neighbor happen to be named Pandora?" I asked with a smile pulling at the corners of my mouth.

"As a matter of fact, she is," he replied.

"Can she be played by Moon Sunny Swartz?" I inquired.

"Oh my God," Abaddon said with a choked laugh.

"But of course," Sean said. "Is there a specific reason why?"

"There is," I replied, unable to hide my glee. "I'd like you to write that Pandora has a disorder... she enjoys humping furniture. Can't seem to stop herself. In public."

Sean threw his head back and laughed. "Seriously?"

"Deadly," I replied.

My brother grabbed his laptop and opened it up. "I'll need until late tonight to get the script ready. Will that work?"

I looked over at Abaddon who wasn't quite sure we were serious. We were.

"Can we use a sound stage at your studio?" I asked.

"You're really going to do this?" he asked.

"You have something better?"

He shook his head. "No. And yes. We can use one of the sound stages. I'll have it completely secured and guarded by our people. How long will we need to shoot this... sitcom?"

"One day. I think we should livestream," I told him. "We gonna gorilla this sucker."

"Go with a typical house interior, a front yard and a community center conference room for the sets," Sean said.

"Got it."

Sean was typing like a madman. "You want a running title?"

"You have one?"

He looked at the computer screen. "Jotted a couple down. We can go with one or come up with something better. I've got *Dastardly Dwellings, Wicked Giggles, Demons Do It Dirty, Demonic Domicile* or *The Wicked Warehouse*. Your call, sis."

My gut knew exactly which one to go with. Nothing in the Immortal world happened without reason. I had a warehouse in my head. If I was going to star in the sitcom that was going to bring the Shitty Whore to her knees, I wanted a warehouse in the dang title. *"The Wicked Warehouse."*

"The Wicked Warehouse it is," Sean said. "Get back to LA and get everything ready. Dad, can you work on hacking into the Demon Network?"

"Can do," Man-mom said.

Lilith clapped her hands together. "Alright! We all have our roles. I'd suggest we get started. Cecily, you need to think long and hard about what you're going to do if you manage to get Pandora to come to you."

I nodded. I already knew what I was going to do.

If I could somehow let the hope out so I could embrace what is repugnant to discover the beauty beneath, there was a chance Pandora could be redeemed. She'd have to serve a *long* sentence for the crimes she'd committed, but the true bad person—or whatever it was—seemed to be the Higher Power.

"I will. I promise," I told Lilith. "You have my word."

CHAPTER TWELVE

THE DAY HAD DAWNED BRIGHT AND SUNNY—LIKE MOST DAYS in LA. However, today was going to be like no other. The cast and crew of *The Wicked Warehouse* were jonesing to go.

Sean had made good on his promise and sent the script the night before. It was as horrifying as promised. He'd apologized repeatedly for the shitty dialogue but laughed like a loon the entire time we'd talked. He was devastated that he couldn't be in the studio to watch the shitshow in person, but for his safety, I'd insisted he stay put. He planned to watch with Lilith and Man-mom as we livestreamed the disaster.

Abaddon was the badass in charge of everything. He'd brought in Demon security. The set was locked down tight. However, if Pandora wanted to get in here, she was one of the very few who could do it.

Sushi was back in wardrobe as our costumer. She was

also doing makeup and hair since there was no way I could pull my human BFF, Jenni, into this Immortal mess.

Ophelia decided to work behind the scenes and direct the episode.

Cher was the head of production, running the sound and light boards and set-dressing for the show along with keeping a close eye on Ophelia. Cher had explained to the Demon that if she punched anyone on the set, she would be in deep shit. While Ophelia thought the rule was unfair, she agreed to the terms.

Uncle Joe was the show's mascot. I was mostly sure he wouldn't show up on film, but asked him to stay out of the shots just in case.

Jonny and Stella had come back to LA and were building the sets. Not only were Stella's knockers machine guns, they also doubled as drills. Her mammary talents were endless.

Corny had been cast as my absent-minded dad. He was a little upset he had to wear clothes, but he went with it when I told him he could bare ass it for the final credits.

Irma was playing my BFF. That was a stretch, but she was thrilled.

Fifi took on the role of my sister. We didn't look a thing alike, she was a blonde Amazon, and I was shorter with dark hair, but no one gave a rat's ass.

Besides building the sets, Jonny was also acting in the show. He was playing my husband. Abaddon had been beyond clear with him that if he touched my rear end or my girls, he'd lose his hands and his junk.

I was playing me—Bitch Goddess Cecily. Of course, as

written, it was nothing like me, but I was an actress. I'd make it work.

The real star of the show was Moon Sunny Swartz. She'd passed out in excitement when I'd explained the role she'd be playing. Sushi had done a bang-up job on Moon's look. My furniture hump-loving buddy sported a wig of raven black hair that hung down to her waist, and her costume was insane. Sushi had gone with Oscar de La Renta. It was stunning and very Pandora. However, the best part was that Moon decided to black-out her two front teeth and used spirit gum to strategically glue on a few large warts. The one on the tip of her nose was killer.

It was a little risky, but we pulled in Bean Gomez as the cinematographer. I found out from Lilith that Bean had been loyal to her, not Pandora. When I'd explained what we were doing, she was all in.

The set was divided into thirds. One-third was a typical suburban living room. One-third was a front yard that one would find in any upper-middle-class neighborhood complete with flowers, manicured bushes, a mailbox and a large plastic pink flamingo—the plastic bird was Irma's idea. No one wanted to hurt her feelings, so we left it. The last third was the interior of the community center—a bland room with a podium, a bunch of gray folding chairs and two tables loaded down with punch, cookies and vodka. Cher thought the vodka was a nice touch.

"We go in ten," Cher shouted, running around like a chicken with her head cut off. My agent was in her element. In her quest to be the best producer alive, she'd done her makeup with extra care. Unfortunately, she hadn't used a mirror. Her lips were blue, and her eyeliner was bright red. She looked diseased... and beautiful.

Standing in the living room set, I took a deep breath. Man-mom was at the safehouse, ready to push the buttons so we would go live on the Demon Network. He was waiting for the go from Abaddon. The title card introduced Pandora as the writer of *The Wicked Warehouse*. Sean had thought that was a move that would piss her off. I agreed. Plus, he didn't want his name anywhere near the contents of the show.

Abaddon approached with a look of concern on his handsome face.

"What?"

"Feeling a little wonky about this," he admitted.

"Join the club," I agreed. "As dangerous as it might be, it's more dangerous if Pandora is on the loose. Lilith isn't safe. Man-mom's not safe and Sean's not safe. None of us are safe. I refuse to let her destroy what's mine anymore."

Abaddon wrapped me in his strong arms and hugged me tight. "Your life was a whole lot less complicated before we crashed into your world."

I hugged him back. "Word. But I wouldn't have you if you freaks hadn't imploded my life. There's no going back. I choose to go forward. Actually, I don't have much of a choice in the matter, so I'm going forward."

He gave me a lopsided smile. "I really, really, really like you, Cecily Bloom."

I raised a brow. "Like? You only *like* me?"

"You ready for me to up the ante?" he questioned. His tone was playful, but his eyes were deadly serious.

"You can't take it back once you say it," I warned him. My body felt like a live wire. The Demon could make me giddy with just a smile. The fact that he wanted to say the three forbidden words made me want to tackle him and play tonsil hockey.

He grinned and tweaked my nose. "I have no intention of taking it back."

The badass Demon, known as Destroyer, loved me, and I loved him. Life didn't come with guarantees. I'd learned that in a big way over the last few weeks. If we succeeded in luring Pandora to the set to put her back in the box—or something along those lines—there was no telling what would go down. I had no intention of biting it, but I'd already neglected telling someone else I'd loved them before they died. Granted, my mom hadn't truly died, but the lesson had been learned. I would beat the beautiful Demon to the punch.

Leaning in, I pressed my lips lightly against his. "I love you, Abaddon."

"I love you more, Cecily," he whispered.

"That's not possible," I told him with a wide grin.

"Is," he countered.

"Not," I shot back.

He laughed. "How about we discuss this later? In bed. Naked."

"Bold," I replied with little shiver of anticipation.

"Is that a yes?"

"It's a resounding yes," I told him.

His wicked grin lit my panties on fire. I pushed him away so I didn't pull a Moon and start humping him in public. "Get away from me. I have to concentrate."

His laugh as he left to check on the progress was music to my ears. My track record with men had always been terrible… until now. All my dreams were going to come true…tonight, naked and in bed. I just had to survive the day.

Moon wandered around practicing her lines. I'd been concerned that the cast would have trouble since we'd only had a ridiculously short amount of time to learn an entire script. My worry had been misplaced. We'd rehearsed for two hours at dawn's crack at my house before coming to the studio. My people had memories like steel traps. The dialogue was horrendous, but that was the point. I couldn't wait until Sean saw Moon in *action*. His descriptions of her getting jiggy with the furniture were mild compared to her usual humping. My brother was in for a gag-worthy treat while watching his embarrassing masterpiece come to life from afar.

"I'm nervous," Irma said, coming up behind me. The Demon was shaking like a leaf. "Think I might puke."

"You'll be fine," I told her, casually backing away. "Nerves means you care, but if you're going to throw up, aim it a Moon during the run. That'll make Pandora lose it."

"Will do," she said as she scurried away to get a final touch-up.

"My liege Bitch Goddess Cecily," Fifi yelled from the

other side of the set. "Would it be okay if I carry grenades? Makes me feel more secure."

I glanced over at Abaddon. His face was a mask of horror. I widened my eyes at him for some input on the explosive matter, but he just shrugged and shook his head.

It was all on me. The question was one of the strangest I'd fielded. "Umm... I guess," I told her. "But under no circumstance are you to use them unless we get attacked. Am I clear?"

"Very!" Fifi shouted. She opened her overcoat, and I gasped. The Succubus was packing at least ten grenades, three swords, a few wicked-sharp daggers and a machine gun. "I'm ready for my close-up!"

"Jesus Hymie Christ," Cher grunted, grabbing the vodka off the prop table and taking a swig. "Forget about the Shitty Whore, that nutjob is going to be the end of all of us." She cupped her hands around her mouth and shouted, "Five minutes, mother humpers."

Corny scurried over. He was wearing underpants—only underpants. "Does this costume work for you?"

"It's not much of a costume," I said. "Is that what Sushi gave you to wear?"

"NO," Sushi shouted. "He has a full costume in the dressing room. The dumbass refuses to put it on."

Corny blushed and got down on his knees. "The pants were strangling my knobs. I can't act if my balls can't breathe. Please, Bitch Goddess Cecily. Let me wear this costume."

Fifi was armed to the teeth. Irma was probably going to

lose her cookies at some point during the show. Did it really matter if Corny was in his tighty-whities?

No. It did not.

"Fine," I said, giving up. "But if you remove them before the final credits, I'll tell Fifi she can use her sword to remove all of the non-PG visuals."

"Harsh," Corny muttered, putting his hands protectively over his privates.

"Take it or leave it," I shot back.

"I'll take it," he said. "You won't regret it. My acting will be stellar because my balls are free."

Abaddon overheard the conversation. "You still think this is a good plan?"

"Actually, no," I said with a laugh. "But if the Shitty Whore shows up, it's worth it."

"The security can double as backup," he said, all business. "I've had the lot cleared. Not one human is present."

"How did you do that?"

"Gas leak," he replied.

"Are you serious?"

He winked. "No, I'm Abaddon or Dick, as you used to be so fond of calling me. The gas leak is fiction, but that's a secret."

"I'm very good at keeping secrets," I promised. A loud boom made me jump as I leaned in to kiss the Demon I loved.

The blast of orange glitter was a surprise. The Immortal who showed up? Not so much.

"Why wasn't I told we were shooting a fucking show?" Candy Vargo shouted.

"Clearly, you were, asshat," Cher said. "Otherwise, you wouldn't be here."

Candy huffed and puffed. She wasn't happy. "Thank goodness for Lilith. If she hadn't told me what you fuckers were doing, I might have missed my shot at stardom."

"What?" I asked, confused.

Candy Vargo rolled her eyes and flipped me off. "You told me I could pole dance on your TV show."

I squinted at her. "Not sure I said those exact words."

She ignored me. "So, I've come to pole dance on your show. Where's the fucking pole?"

"Coming right up," Stella said, snapping her fingers and producing a shiny stripper pole right smack in the middle of the living room set. She drilled it into the floor with her boobs. That DIY move elicited applause. Because, you know... boobs.

"Now you're talking," Candy said, admiring the pole. "Sushi, you got a costume for me?"

"No," she said flatly.

"No worries. I brought my own."

The Keeper of Fate removed her sweatpants and baggy sweater. Underneath, she wore an old-timey, purple polka-dot swimsuit with a bustle. It was the antithesis of what one would wear while sliding—or falling, in Candy's case—on a pole. Sushi groaned in disgust and walked away. The outfit was a tragedy of a spandex dress with a big pink ruffle on the butt. Candy pulled out a red swim cap from her cleavage and put it on. Her black socks and mismatched tennis shoes were the icing on top of the poop cake.

"How do I look?"

"Great," I lied. "I'm not sure you have any lines."

"Don't matter," she assured me. "I'll be on the pole the entire time. If I think of something interesting to say, I'll just ad lib."

"Awesome."

"PLACES," Cher shouted.

Bean was behind the camera, ready to roll. Ophelia, who'd found a beret somewhere, was in her director's chair. It wasn't her best look, but she had Candy's swimsuit and Corny's underpants beat. Uncle Joe hovered in the air above the camera, his hands clasped in delight. Stella was with Cher at the light and sound boards.

Abaddon called my dad to start the livestream. Shit was getting real.

Cher let out a whistle. "Places every one!"

Corny sat down on the couch in his grundies. Both Moon and Fifi were waiting for their cues on the upstage side of the front door hidden from view. Irma was perched on the loveseat, looking very green in the face. I made a mental note to keep a healthy distance. Jonny sat down next to Corny on the couch. I went to my mark at the entryway to the kitchen. Candy Vargo hopped up on her pole, fell off, cussed like a sailor and tried again. This was going to be interesting.

"Quiet on the set," Cher bellowed.

"Lights! Camera! Action, bitches," Ophelia called out.

It was all I could do not to laugh.

The theme music blasted through the speakers. It was catchy and cheesy. The canned laugh track was positively

cringey. It was perfection. The prerecorded opener that
Sean had made was next.

"Live from studio B at Keystone Studios in sunny LA, it's
The Wicked Warehouse. Written entirely by the Shitty Whore
aka Pandora! Sit back. Relax. And enjoy the show!" Sean's
voice boomed through the soundstage loud and clear. If
there was any doubt about where we were, it had been
quashed.

And the shitshow began...

Corny stood up and stretched. "Well, now, kiddledoo-
dles. I think it's time you people move out of my house and
get your own places. You Demons are too old to be living
with your pappy!"

"That's funny, pops!" Jonny shouted, standing up and
flexing his muscles—for a full minute. I didn't recall that
move from the script, but there wasn't a stripper pole in the
show, either. "I own this house."

Canned laughter.

Corny smacked himself in the head and guffawed.
"That's right. I forgot."

"No worries, pops," Jonny assured him. "You're the
reason shampoo bottles have directions!"

Corny and Jonny high-fived. The laugh track made the
moment *special.*

"Goddammit," Candy bellowed. "The fucking pole
should have been greased. Pretty sure all the skin on my
inner thighs is gone."

We ignored the outburst and kept going.

"Demontastic!" Irma shouted, then burped loudly. I was

sure she was going to blow her cookies. "Did you hear about Pandora?"

"No," I said. "What about Pandora? I've been so busy being Bitch Goddess Cecily, I almost forgot about the old hag."

The canned laugh track almost made me laugh. Cher wasn't messing around.

Irma said her next line while fully belching again. It was gross. "I heard the Shitty Whore's gene pool needs more chlorine!"

"Funny," Jonny said, slapping his thighs. "I heard she's weapons-grade stupid."

"Demontastic!" Irma shouted. She burped three more times before she lurched forward and puked all over Jonny.

"What, and I cannot stress enough, the fuck?" Jonny shrieked.

That wasn't in the script.

Irma began to gag again, then sprinted off the stage. Jonny followed closely behind her, screeching like a banshee.

Again, not in the script. I half expected Ophelia to yell cut, but we were live. There was no stopping. We were about to enter the unknown. I was here for the ride. Abaddon, on the other hand, appeared horrified. He obviously hadn't read the script. The worst was yet to come...

"Oh wow," I said, pulling it out of my butt since two of the actors bailed. "Did you hear the doorbell, Pops?"

"What?" Corny asked, wildly confused.

Out of the corner of my eye, I saw Cher lunge for the sound board. The doorbell effect came through the speakers along with the canned laughter and the fake applause.

"I'll get it!" I said, moving quickly to the door. The script was out the window now. We were missing half the cast.

"Son of a bitch," Candy griped, falling off the pole and hitting the ground with a thud. "Fucking pole." She yanked it out of the ground and tossed it over to the front yard set. She then walked over to Corny, popped the elastic of his underpants and sat down on the couch. "Let's get this party started!"

As I swung open the door, Fifi entered and took a bow. Cher was on it. The applause track came on. "Hello, my liege Bitch Goddess Cecily's sister. I'm back from the war!"

"Don't you mean the store?" I asked, trying to help her out.

"Shite," she announced in her outdoor voice. "I meant the store."

"Demontastic," Irma shouted from the bathroom that was located at the far-left side of the set.

"My pants are ruined," Jonny shouted from the dressing rooms. "I can't fucking believe this."

"Where are they?" Fifi whispered, looking around.

"Irma puked on Jonny. They left," I said under my breath as I took the shopping bags from her hands.

Fifi had practiced her lines diligently. She was clearly thrown that we'd gone off-script and was struggling to adapt to the new scenario. To calm herself, she pulled out two grenades. Cher blasted the laugh track to lessen the impact of explosives on the set. "I bought the fixin's for nachos! Anyone hungry?"

Uncle Joe was in hysterics. Even Abaddon had a slight crooked grin on his face. Ophelia and Stella were into it, and Cher was sweating like a hooker at confession. Only Bean remained professional.

"Oh my!" I exclaimed. "I do believe someone else is at the door."

"You do?" Corny asked, more confused than ever. "I didn't hear the doorbell. Oh my GOD. Do you think I've gone deaf? Maybe if I take off my underpants, I'll be able to hear better."

Before I had the chance to tell him hell to the no, Candy Vargo electrocuted him. Corny slapped out the fire and pouted. At least he was still clothed.

"What the fuck is going on?" Cher muttered as she frantically pressed buttons. Unfortunately, the theme song came back on. I just went with it.

"Yep, I have a bad feeling about who might be on the other side of the door," I told the crowd with a shudder. "I hope it's not Pandora."

"In the script, it says it's Pandora, my liege Bitch Goddess Cecily's sister," Fifi assured me. "If it's not her, I shall lob a grenade at the intruder, flay the skin from their body, behead them, then shove their entrails down their throat."

"That is a *really* bad idea, sister," I said, giving her the eyeball.

Cher hit the laugh track.

"I'll bet you five hundred million dollars and twenty cents that it's the Shitty Whore," Candy Vargo announced.

Closing my eyes for a hot sec, I hoped she wasn't serious.

I wasn't paying her five hundred million dollars and twenty cents. I also hoped it was Moon behind the door and not the real Shitty Whore.

Only one way to find out.

I opened the door and Moon sauntered into the room. I heaved a sigh of relief. She tossed her long hair and sneered. It was pretty darn good. "Half the Demon! All the taste!" she shouted.

"What the hell was that?" Candy Vargo asked.

"It's my catchphrase," Moon snapped. "Nice furniture, Bitch Goddess Cecily."

"Oh no, you don't," I cried out as I tried to block her from fornicating with the couch.

"Melts in your Demon," she hissed as she shoved me out of the way. "Not in your hand."

"For the love of everything that sucks ass," Candy said with an eye roll. "Was that another catchphrase?"

"It was," Corny confirmed. "I wasn't given a catchphrase. I feel gypped. I do have a line that got skipped because Irma emptied the contents of her stomach. Shall I say it?"

"Yep," Candy said, hopping off the couch as Moon began to seduce it.

Corny also moved off the couch, cleared his throat, and then slid his underpants slightly down. No junk was showing, but it was close. "Alright then, here's what I know. An apple a day will keep the doctor away if you aim it expertly and nail the bastard between the eyes."

Cher hit the laugh track. Everyone else groaned.

Moon started with a slow hump. She was working up to

the biggies. "Pops, I'm still deciding if you're the weakest link or the missing link."

Candy wasn't having it. "You leave that mostly naked fucker alone, *Pandora*," she snapped. "Pops might be missing some gray matter, but you're a sentient fucking menstrual cramp."

Moon's eyes narrowed to slits as she straddled the couch and undulated like a freaking porn star. None of this was in the script. "Oh yeah? Well, you look smarter in pictures."

Cher was in a tizzy. She hit the laugh track, the boo track and the theme song.

"Weak," Candy Vargo commented, punctuating it with a raised middle finger. "I'm gonna go out on a limb and say your family tree doesn't have enough branches."

Cher nailed the applause track on that one. Candy Vargo looked right into the camera and took a bow. Sean had to be losing his shit. I knew I was.

Moon was getting seriously jiggy with the couch now. It was hard to watch. "The closest you'll come to a brainstorm is a drizzle," she panted.

Candy laughed. "Does your ass know about all the shit that comes out of your mouth, Pandora? Because if it did, I'm gonna guess it's pretty jealous."

"Demontastic," Irma shouted from the bathroom.

"Are there any other pants for me to wear?" Jonny called out from the dressing room. "These are fucked. I can't get the puke smell out of them."

I stole a quick glance at Ophelia as Sushi hightailed it back to Jonny. Ophelia's mouth was wide open in shock. I was just surprised that she hadn't jumped into the fray and doled out a few left hooks.

Moon was living her best life. The whole cast and crew were speechless—even Candy Vargo—who was never at a loss for words—just stared in appalled shock. Honestly, it was kind of traumatizing.

"I am Pandora," Moon shouted. "I find furniture arousing. Couches are the best, but armchairs and bathroom caddies will do in a pinch. I am Pandora. I eat babies for breakfast."

"Wait. What?" I choked out. That was definitely not in the script.

"Not me," Moon said for clarification. "Pandora."

"Oh my God. Is that true?" I asked, getting close to pulling an Irma and tossing my cookies.

"Nope," Moon said. "I just thought it would be insulting."

"Like you fuckin' a couch as Pandora isn't insulting enough?" Candy Vargo asked.

Corny chimed in. "While I think all forms of expression are beautiful, like nudity and banging inanimate objects, eating babies is a little much."

"Well, Pops," Fifi said, trying her damnedest to stay in character. "I think it's time for me to go back to the war."

"The store," I corrected her.

"Shite. My bad. The store," she shouted as she smacked her head in frustration and sprinted out the front door.

Cher hit the laugh track, the sigh track and the screaming track. I hadn't realized there was a screaming track. We could have used that a few times earlier.

Moon was, unfortunately, close to completion. It had gotten really ugly.

And that's when it got uglier.

We'd succeeded.

The real Pandora had arrived.

It was time to deal with the box... or die trying.

CHAPTER THIRTEEN

AN ICY WIND TORE THROUGH THE ROOM, UPENDING THE SET pieces and all of the furniture. Pandora hadn't come alone. She had twenty flaming assholes with her, and she was irate. Her normally gorgeous alabaster skin was a mottled red. Her gown was wrinkled and torn, and her eyes were manic. She'd clearly been in hiding and it hadn't treated her well.

"How dare you," she roared. "You will pay. Oh," she added with a laugh that verged on hysteria. "Don't worry about your backup security. I killed them."

Abaddon's growl of fury made my blood run cold. The strikes against Pandora were too many to count.

The Demon hadn't changed much. Her crazy was showing, and she was delusional. The Shitty Whore was still stunning with an evil iciness to her. She was viciously insane and lacked a conscience, but there was no discounting how smart she was. Her sadistic cunning had gotten her through millions of years.

"You've got it all wrong, Pandora," I said flatly as I raised my hands in the air and produced two fire swords. "Your unhinged mind has it backwards. You're going to pay."

Her flaming assholes snarled and bared their teeth. The searing heat coming from their hulking bodies stank like sulfur and made my stomach roil. The green fire with icy blue sparks covered their bodies popping and crackling ominously.

Pandora and her people were on one side of the large soundstage. Me and my people were on the other. My posse were no slouches. We were outnumbered, but we were a deadly crew. Abaddon had gone all badass and was glowing dangerously. His eyes blazed red, and his purple fire sword appeared in his hand. His presence made the flaming assholes nervous. They kept their eyes glued to the Destroyer. Too bad, so sad for them... there were several of us almost as deadly as Abaddon.

Fifi morphed into a hulking, six-foot monster with razor-sharp fangs. With a grenade in each hand, she looked like a nightmare come to life.

Cher had ripped off her shirt and downy white wings burst from her back. She wielded a glowing golden stick. It looked like a massive dildo. Ophelia had her purple fire sword and was no longer sporting a beret. The Demon was as deadly as advertised.

"Stella," I commanded. "Transport Uncle Joe and Bean. NOW. Get them out of here."

Without a word, she obeyed. They disappeared in a mist of her shimmering black dust.

Jonny came sprinting out of the dressing room, minus

the puke pants. He'd morphed into a monster over eight feet tall complete with claws and fangs. It was a chilling look, and he wore it well.

He also wasn't fucking around.

When he opened his jaws, it appeared unhinged, like something out of a zombie movie. It was insane and gave the flaming assholes pause.

Sushi the Succubus, no shrinking violet, walked front and center, wearing a white tux and patent leather red shoes. Her razor-sharp fangs were extended, and she looked the flaming assholes up and down like they were pieces of meat, and she was going to a barbecue. I had no clue if she was about to break her nine-hundred-year celibacy streak, but the threat was there.

Corny Crackers was naked and holding knitting needles. If I hadn't seen him behead flaming assholes with his hobby utensils, I would have been concerned. I wasn't. He was a master with his wool tools. Moon was still humping the couch which almost sent Pandora over the edge. However, my horny buddy now had an enchanted sword in each hand, compliments of Fifi. It was a disturbing picture, but it was what it was. Moon was nuts, but she was mine. I'd defend her till the death.

But they weren't the last of my crew...

With a shriek so high pitched I was sure I'd burst an eardrum, Irma Stoutwagon joined the posse. She reminded me of a rabid Tasmanian Devil on crack... or maybe a pissed off honey badger on a week-long cocaine bender. She was out of control.

Everyone took a wary step back except Candy Vargo.

Candy was the OG of badasses. The Keeper of Fate didn't morph into anything. She wasn't glowing. She had no weapon in her hand. Candy simply crossed her arms over her chest and glared at Pandora. As nutty as it seemed, she was the scariest Immortal in the room. Her confidence was killer. Pandora studiously avoided eye contact with her.

"No one makes fun at my expense," Pandora bellowed as spittle flew from her lips.

I heard the whir of the camera and realized we were still being live-streamed. Bean hadn't turned off the camera. I was going to turn that happy accident into a win.

"And no one kills the Goddess Lilith and gets away with it," I shot back.

"I didn't kill the bitch," Pandora screamed. "You have no proof."

Cher laughed. Sushi laughed. Abaddon didn't move a muscle. The rest of my people laughed along. They had no clue why they were laughing, but it made the situation at hand more ominous.

"Stop it," Pandora shrieked. "NOW."

"You want proof?" I ground out. "I'll give you and the Demon world proof."

Silently and with no fanfare, Candy Vargo, Abaddon and Fifi surrounded me for protection. Without a moment to lose, I closed my eyes and projected the demise of my mother by Pandora's hand. The shitty whore was speechless as the holograms played out in front of her... and all of her people tuning into the Demon Network. I hated that Man-mom and Lilith were watching, but that was beyond my control. I could only hope they would turn off the feed.

Pandora could no longer refute that she'd thrown the massive fireball that had ended the Goddess Lilith's Immortal life. Her flaming assholes grew uncomfortable and began to mutter amongst themselves. It was looking less and less like hand-to-hand combat was going to occur. That was a plus. Losing any of my friends because they were fighting my battles would devastate me.

"Attack," Pandora commanded. "Kill them."

Her flunkies didn't move.

"I am your GODDESS," she screamed. "Do my bidding, or you will die."

They stood motionless. The flaming assholes were still dangerous, but their leader had screwed them over. I wasn't sure if she was in more danger from them or if we were. One by one, they morphed back into a human-looking form. One by one, they turned their back on her as if to shun her existence. Her shriek of fury shook the building at its foundation. Pandora's eyes turned black, and a haze of pure evil swirled around her. It was difficult to breathe. I took short shallow breaths so I didn't pass out. The depraved Goddess raised her hands over her head and created a massive fireball. As she threw it at the men she considered traitors, Candy Vargo flicked her pinky finger and dropped a shield around them. The fireball hit the barrier with a thunderous explosion, then the blast flew back at Pandora. She screamed in agony as her viciousness backfired.

Note to self—never ever get on Candy Vargo's bad side.

As Pandora rolled around on the floor, trying to douse the flames, her eyes darted wildly around the set like a cornered animal. Her body convulsed as if she was having a seizure. It was difficult to feel compassion for the vile woman, but a small part of me did. It was clear her power was depleted. She'd have put out the flames and transported away if she'd had any real strength left.

If the Higher Power had truly put the box inside her, her heinous behaviors were the result of that one tragic action. While it couldn't excuse what she'd done over the millions of years she'd been alive, it was a piece of the catastrophic puzzle that had shaped her.

There needed to be two Goddesses of the Darkness to keep the balance. I was one and, sadly, she was the other. Letting her die wasn't on the table. Retracting my swords, I waved my hands and doused the flames. Part of me wanted to watch her burn for her sins, but a bigger part of me couldn't let it happen. Instead, I made the compassionate choice.

Slowly, I walked to her. I held up my hand when Abaddon and Candy Vargo tried to interfere. "I've got this."

I could hear the tension in Abaddon's voice. "As you wish."

"Fuckin' badass," Candy Vargo said. "Real deal."

I wanted to prove her correct. I would prove her correct.

Pandora lay in a pathetic heap on the cold cement floor. When she noticed my approach, she tried to crawl away.

The tides had changed. It was time to use the key.

"Don't touch me," she hissed with psychotic rage. "NO ONE TOUCHES ME. Ever. You are a lowly nothing—a piece of shit beneath my shoe. I am Pandora, Goddess of the Darkness. If you touch me, I will destroy you."

I forced myself to remember that at one time she was good. There was very little evidence of that anymore, but if all of our findings were correct, hope still lived inside the wretched woman. If I could get to it, she might be free of the evil and chaos the Higher Power had *gifted* her. She would still pay for her sins, but it might afford her some peace.

"The truth can shift," I said, speaking the key aloud. "In the Darkness, the seed of hope awaits. Behind every smile lies a dark secret. What you see is rarely what you get. Some bridges are meant to be burned. Embrace what is repugnant to discover the beauty that lies beneath. Often the answer has been in front of you the entire time."

"Stop it," she snarled. "Rubbish. You know nothing of what you speak. Do *not* touch me. I will make you regret it."

The key wasn't supposed to be used to lock Pandora away in a box. The key had been meant to save her. The key was to open the box and let the hope seep out. It was to let the box out of Pandora and free her from the evil that had been her prison for so long. Both of the Goddesses had been tested horridly by the Higher Power. In the end, both had failed.

This test wasn't the end for me. It was the beginning. I could create change by embracing the repugnant to discover the beauty that lies beneath. My gut told me the answer was in the embrace.

"Look at me," I told her sternly.

She refused. It didn't matter. She had ears. The Demon would hear what I had to say.

"The truth is shifting. Your people no longer have faith

in you because you have committed the vilest sin a Goddess can commit. You killed Lilith."

She raised her head and glared at me.

"Your smile belies the tragedy that lives inside you," I said. "You are Pandora's box. The box is you."

She reached out, her fingers splayed in a move I'd seen her use when shooting electricity at her foes. With her power zapped, nothing happened, not even a piteous spark. In her frustration, the Demon Goddess spit in my direction.

Her reaction meant I was probably on the right track, so I kept going. "Burn the bridge that you've walked on for so long. It's the past. The only thing left in Pandora's box is hope. I can help you let it out."

"Fuck you," she ground out.

"I'd rather not," I replied.

Her lackeys laughed. The irate glare she shot their way didn't affect them. They were done. She knew it, and they knew it.

"Don't let your pride be the sin that destroys you," I said calmly.

"It already has," she screamed. "Let me out. Let me leave. I'll not bother you again."

I shook my head. "Not the way it works. Embrace what is repugnant to discover the beauty that lies beneath."

Getting down on the floor next to the broken Goddess, I wrapped my arms around her. She fought me tooth and nail, but she was no match for a Goddess at full strength. As I hugged her tight against my body, she began to sob. It pulled at my heart, and I held her even tighter. In my arms was the woman who had killed my mother—the woman who had done her best to destroy me.

Pandora's hatred for me might never go away. My hatred for her might last for eternity, but it didn't outweigh my pity for what the Higher Power had done. Who knew? In time, I might even learn to forgive her.

I felt the tendril of hope heat both of our bodies. A golden glow surrounded us and danced over our skin. The sensation was glorious. Pandora's eyes rolled into the back of her head as she went limp in my arms.

Oh, holy Hell. Was she dead? Had I killed her? That hadn't been the plan. Killing the Goddess would make me no better than her, regardless of my intention. To top it off, we were still live on the Demon Network.

Frantically, I searched for a pulse and let out an audible sigh of relief. Pandora's heartbeat was steady and strong. The Demon Goddess wasn't dead.

There was applause, and I couldn't tell if it was the Demon's or one of Cher's audio effects. I let out a soft squeal when the glowing enchantment lifted us both off the ground and suspended us high in the air. A summer-scented breeze gently wafted through the scene before the golden light surrounding us went from warm and gentle to nuclear blinding.

I shielded my eyes as we floated back to the ground cradled in the breeze and landed softly. When the light diminished, Pandora's eyes shot open and bored into mine. She appeared desperate and terrified.

"It's okay," I whispered. "You're okay."

Her smile was fleeting as she began to fade. My pulse

kicked up a notch as I held her tighter in the hopes that she wouldn't disappear. This wasn't a transport. She wasn't escaping. No. This was something I couldn't have expected. Pandora was literally fading into nothing.

"What's happening?" I cried out.

Candy and Abaddon rushed over.

"Help me help her," I begged as Pandora grew more transparent.

"I told you not to touch me," she whispered brokenly as she faded into nothing.

"Where the hell is she?" Abaddon ground out, glancing around wildly.

"Hold that thought," Candy said as she began to glow. "I just need a sec here."

No one said a word as the Keeper of Fate glowed so brightly we had to look away. She chanted in a language I'd never heard, and diamond-like crystals rained down from the ceiling, covering every surface on the sound stage.

It stopped as abruptly as it began.

"Fuck me," Candy Vargo said with a surprised chuckle. "Can't quite explain it. She's gone but she ain't dead."

"Then where is she?" Abaddon demanded.

Candy shrugged. "Not sure, but it ain't far."

I stood up and dusted the crystals off my clothes. In a move that shocked everyone, Pandora's henchmen got down on their knees and bowed to me. "All hail, Bitch Goddess Cecily," the Demon in the front shouted.

The others repeated it.

"Wasn't expecting that," I muttered, keeping an eye open for any sign of Pandora. If anything would bring her out of hiding, I would assume that her people swearing fealty to me would do it.

"Let me out," Pandora begged in a weak and haggard voice.

I whipped around and produced my fire swords. Abaddon followed suit, his expression confused but ready for a fight.

I didn't see Pandora anywhere.

"What's wrong?" Abaddon asked. "Did you see something?"

I shook my head. "Didn't you hear her?"

"Hear what?" he asked, scanning the room.

"It was Pandora," I told him. "She said, let me out."

His brow dipped as his gaze met mine. "I didn't hear anything."

"Neither did I," Candy Vargo said, looking concerned. "But I believe you. I can still feel the shitty whore close by. Try answering her."

I swallowed the knot of anxiety in my throat then asked, "Pandora?"

"Yes." The relief in her voice was palpable. "You can hear me. Good. Now, let me the hell out!"

I had no idea what she was talking about. I kept looking around the stage to see if I could pinpoint where her voice was coming from, but to no avail. "Where are you?"

"I warned you, and you wouldn't listen," she hissed. "Now, you have to find a way to let me out or else."

I looked at Candy and Abaddon for help. They both still looked bemused. "Don't you hear her?"

Both shook their heads.

I glanced around the room at the other Demons. "Did any of you hear her?"

The answer was no. No one heard her except me.

"You shouldn't have touched me," she said in a flat tone. "I warned you, and now you have to pay."

My breathing came in short jerky spurts as realization hit me like a ton of bricks thrown at my head. Hard. My knees gave out, and I dropped to the floor. Abaddon squatted down beside me and gently pushed my wild hair out of my face.

"I know where she is," I choked out raggedly.

He waited.

I clutched at my chest. "She's in me." I shook my head in denial even as the truth consumed me. "I'm Pandora's box."

Abaddon stood up, slashed his hands through the air, and blew up the far end of the sound stage. "Motherfucker," he bellowed.

I turned to the Keeper of Fate. "What do I do?"

She inhaled slowly and blew it out on a loud woosh. "We're gonna have to make a trip to the Higher Power and get this shit worked out once and for all."

I'd gone from being an unemployed actress to a Goddess who had another Goddess stuck inside her. I'd found my mother. I'd found the love of my life. I was accepted by my people. It looked like I'd be acquiring some of Pandora's people. I had a shitload to live for.

I extended my hand to Abaddon. He was red in the face and still fuming. If I was going to meet the Higher Power, I wanted him by my side. "Will you come with me?"

He nodded jerkily and clasped my hand in his. "There is

no place in the Universe I'd rather be than with you. I'll be by your side until the end of time."

"I love you," I whispered.

"I love you more."

"Not possible," I told him with a sad smile.

"Let's call it even," he replied.

"Deal."

The Keeper of Fate placed her hands on our shoulders. "You ready?"

"No, I'm not ready, but that won't stop me," I said. "Let's get this party started."

Candy nodded. My people cheered and applauded. Pandora's former followers did as well.

Then, in a blast of orange crystals, the three of us exited stage left, so to speak. We were on to the next show. I had no clue how the episode would end, but I was determined to get Pandora out of me. The alternative was unacceptable.

I had three choices. Do it. Don't do it. Or, do the fuck out of it.

I chose the last one. And I played to win.

The End... for now

DO YOU WANT TO KNOW WHAT HAPPENS NEXT? GO HERE TO order the next book, *Blaze of Our Lives.*

MORE IN THE GOOD TO THE LAST DEMON SERIES

ORDER BOOK 5 NOW!

EXCERPT: THE WRITE HOOK

BOOK DESCRIPTION

THE WRITE HOOK

Midlife is full of surprises. Not all of them are working for me.

At forty-two I've had my share of ups and downs. Relatively normal, except when the definition of normal changes... drastically.

NYT Bestselling Romance Author: Check
Amazing besties: Check
Lovely home: Check
Pet cat named Thick Stella who wants to kill me: Check
Wacky Tabacky Dealing Aunt: Check
Cheating husband banging the weather girl on our kitchen table: Check
Nasty Divorce: Oh yes
Characters from my novels coming to life: Umm... yes
Crazy: Possibly

Four months of wallowing in embarrassed depression should be enough. I'm beginning to realize that no one is who they seem to be, and my life story might be spinning out of my control. It's time to take a shower, put on a bra, and wear something other than sweatpants. Difficult, but doable.

With my friends—real and imaginary—by my side, I need to edit my life before the elusive darkness comes for all of us.

The plot is no longer fiction. It's my reality, and I'm writing a happy ever after no matter what. I just have to find the *write hook.*

CHAPTER 1

"I didn't leave that bowl in the sink," I muttered to no one as I stared in confusion at the blue piece of pottery with milk residue in the bottom. "Wait. Did I?"

Slowly backing away, I ran my hands through my hair that hadn't seen a brush in days—possibly longer—and decided that I wasn't going to think too hard about it. Thinking led to introspective thought, which led to dealing with reality, and that was a no-no.

Reality wasn't my thing right now.

Maybe I'd walked in my sleep, eaten a bowl of cereal, then politely put the bowl in the sink. It was possible.

"That has to be it," I announced, walking out of the kitchen and avoiding all mirrors and any glass where I could catch a glimpse of myself.

It was time to get to work. Sadly, books didn't write themselves.

"I can do this. I have to do this." I sat down at my desk

and made sure my posture didn't suck. I was fully aware it would suck in approximately five minutes, but I wanted to start out right. It would be a bad week to throw my back out. "Today, I'll write ten thousand words. They will be coherent. I will not mistakenly or on purpose make a list of the plethora of ways I would like to kill Darren. He's my past. Beheading him is illegal. I'm far better than that. On a more positive note, my imaginary muse will show his pony-tailed, obnoxious ass up today, and I won't play Candy Jelly Crush until the words are on the page."

Two hours later...

Zero words. However, I'd done three loads of laundry—sweatpants, t-shirts and underwear—and played Candy Jelly Crush until I didn't have any more lives. As pathetic as I'd become, I hadn't sunk so low as to purchase new lives. That would mean I'd hit rock bottom. Of course, I was precariously close, evidenced by my cussing out of the Jelly Queen for ten minutes, but I didn't pay for lives. I considered it a win.

I'd planned on folding the laundry but decided to vacuum instead. I'd fold the loads by Friday. It was Tuesday. That was reasonable. If they were too wrinkled, I'd simply wash them again. No biggie. After the vacuuming was done, I rearranged my office for thirty minutes. I wasn't sure how to Feng Shui, but after looking it up on my phone, I gave it a half-assed effort.

Glancing around at my handiwork, I nodded. "Much better. If the surroundings are aligned correctly, the words will flow magically. I hope."

Two hours later...

"Mother humper," I grunted as I pushed my monstrosity of a bed from one side of the bedroom to the other. "This weighs a damn ton."

I'd burned all the bedding seven weeks ago. The bonfire had been cathartic. I'd taken pictures as the five hundred thread count sheets had gone up in flame. I'd kept the comforter. I'd paid a fortune for it. It had been thoroughly saged and washed five times. Even though there was no trace of Darren left in the bedroom, I'd been sleeping in my office.

The house was huge, beautiful… and mine—a gorgeously restored Victorian where I'd spent tons of time as a child. It had an enchanted feel to it that I adored. I didn't need such an enormous abode, but I loved the location—the middle of nowhere. The internet was iffy, but I solved that by going into town to the local coffee shop if I had something important to download or send.

Darren, with the wandering pecker, thought he would get a piece of the house. He was wrong. I'd inherited it from my whackadoo grandmother and great-aunt Flip. My parents hadn't always been too keen on me spending so much time with Granny and Aunt Flip growing up, but I adored the two old gals so much they'd relented. Since I spent a lot of time in an imaginary dream world, my mom and dad were delighted when I related to actual people— even if they were left of center.

Granny and Flip made sure the house was in my name only—nontransferable and non-sellable. It was stipulated that I had to pass it to a family member or the Historical Society when I died. Basically, I had life rights. It was as if

Granny and Aunt Flip had known I would waste two decades of my life married to a jackhole who couldn't keep his salami in his pants and would need someplace to live. God rest Granny's insane soul. Aunt Flip was still kicking, although I hadn't seen her in a few years.

Aunt Flip put the K in kooky. She'd bought a cottage in the hills about an hour away and grew medicinal marijuana —before it was legal. The old gal was the black sheep of the family and preferred her solitude and her pot to company. She hadn't liked Darren a bit. She and Granny both had worn black to my wedding. Everyone had been appalled— even me—but in the end, it made perfect sense. I had to hand it to the old broads. They'd been smarter than me by a long shot. And the house? It had always been my charmed haven in the storm.

Even though there were four spare bedrooms plus the master suite, I chose my office. It felt safe to me.

Thick Stella preferred my office, and I needed to be around something that had a heartbeat. It didn't matter that Thick Stella was bitchy and swiped at me with her deadly kitty claws every time I passed her. I loved her. The feeling didn't seem mutual, but she hadn't left me for a twenty-three-year-old with silicone breast implants and huge, bright white teeth.

"Thick Stella, do you think Sasha should wear red to her stepmother's funeral?" I asked as I plopped down on my newly Feng Shuied couch and narrowly missed getting gouged by my cat. "Yes or no? Hiss at me if it's a yes. Growl at me if it's a no."

Thick Stella had a go at her privates. She was useless.

"That wasn't an answer." I grabbed my laptop from my desk. Deciding it was too dangerous to sit near my cat, I settled for the love seat. The irony of the piece of furniture I'd chosen didn't escape me.

"I think she should wear red," I told Thick Stella, who didn't give a crap what Sasha wore. "Her stepmother was an asshat, and it would show fabu disrespect."

Typing felt good. Getting lost in a story felt great. I dressed Sasha in a red Prada sheath, then had her behead her ex-husband with a dull butter knife when he and his bimbo showed up unexpectedly to pay their respects at the funeral home. It was a bloodbath. Putting Sasha in red was an excellent move. The blood matched her frock to a T.

Quickly rethinking the necessary murder, I moved the scene of the decapitation to the empty lobby of the funeral home. It would suck if I had to send Sasha to prison. She hadn't banged Damien yet, and everyone was eagerly awaiting the sexy buildup—including me. It was the fourth book in the series, and it was about time they got together. The sexual tension was palpable.

"What in the freaking hell?" I snapped my laptop shut and groaned. "Sasha doesn't have an ex-husband. I can't do this. I've got nothing." Where was my muse hiding? I needed the elusive imaginary idiot if I was going to get any writing done. "Chauncey, dammit, where are you?"

"My God, you're loud, Clementine," a busty, beautiful woman dressed in a deep purple Regency gown said with an eye roll.

She was seated on the couch next to Thick Stella, who barely acknowledged her. My cat attacked strangers and friends. Not today. My fat feline simply glanced over at the intruder and yawned. The cat was a traitor.

Forget the furry betrayer. How in the heck did the woman get into my house—not to mention my office—without me seeing her enter? For a brief moment, I wondered if she'd banged my husband too but pushed the sordid thought out of my head. She looked to be close to thirty—too old for the asshole.

"Who are you?" I demanded, holding my laptop over my head as a weapon.

If I threw it and it shattered, I would be screwed. I couldn't remember the last time I'd backed it up. If I lost the measly, somewhat disjointed fifty thousand words I'd written so far, I'd have to start over. That wouldn't fly with my agent or my publisher.

"Don't be daft," the woman replied. "It's rather unbecoming. May I ask a question?"

"No, you may not," I shot back, trying to place her.

She was clearly a nutjob. The woman was rolling up on thirty but had the vernacular of a seventy-year-old British society matron. She was dressed like she'd walked off the set of a film starring Emma Thompson. Her blonde hair shone to the point of absurdity and was twisted into an elaborate up-do. Wispy tendrils framed her perfectly heart-shaped face. Her sparkling eyes were lavender, enhanced by the over-the-top gown she wore.

Strangely, she was vaguely familiar. I just couldn't remember how I knew her.

"How long has it been since you attended to your hygiene?" she inquired.

Putting my laptop down and picking up a lamp, I eyed her. I didn't care much for the lamp or her question. I had been thinking about Marie Condo-ing my life, and the lamp didn't bring me all that much joy. If it met its demise by use of self-defense, so be it. "I don't see how that's any of your business, lady. What I'd suggest is that you leave. Now. Or else I'll call the police. Breaking and entering is a crime."

She laughed. It sounded like freaking bells. Even though she was either a criminal or certifiable, she was incredibly charming.

"Oh dear," she said, placing her hand delicately on her still heaving, milky-white bosom. "You are so silly. The constable knows quite well that I'm here. He advised me to come."

"The constable?" I asked, wondering how far off her rocker she was.

She nodded coyly. "Most certainly. We're all terribly concerned."

I squinted at her. "About my hygiene?"

"That, amongst other things," she confirmed. "Darling girl, you are not an ace of spades or, heaven forbid, an adventuress. Unless you want to be an ape leader, I'd recommend bathing."

"Are you right in the head?" I asked, wondering where I'd left my damn cell phone. It was probably in the laundry room. I was going to be murdered by a nutjob, and I'd lost my chance to save myself because I'd been playing Candy Jelly Crush. The headline would be horrifying—*Homeless-looking, Hygiene-free Paranormal Romance Author Beheaded by Victorian Psycho.*

If I lived through the next hour, I was deleting the game for good.

"I think it would do wonders for your spirit if you donned a nice tight corset and a clean chemise," she suggested, skillfully ignoring my question. "You must pull yourself together. Your behavior is dicked in the nob."

I sat down and studied her. My about-to-be-murdered radar relaxed a tiny bit, but I kept the lamp clutched tightly in my hand. My gut told me she wasn't going to strangle me. Of course, I could be mistaken, but Purple Gal didn't seem violent—just bizarre. Plus, the lamp was heavy. I could knock her ladylike ass out with one good swing.

How in the heck did I know her? College? Grad School? The grocery store? At forty-two, I'd met a lot of people in my life. Was she with the local community theater troop? I was eighty-six percent sure she wasn't here to off me. However, I'd been wrong about life-altering events before— like not knowing my husband was boffing someone young enough to have been our daughter.

"What language are you speaking?" I spotted a pair of scissors on my desk. If I needed them, it was a quick move to grab them. I'd never actually killed anyone except in ficti-tious situations, but there was a first time for everything.

Pulling an embroidered lavender hankey from her cleav-age, she clutched it and twisted it in her slim fingers. "Clementine, *you* should know."

"I'm at a little disadvantage here," I said, fascinated by the batshit crazy woman who'd broken into my home. "You seem to know my name, but I don't know yours."

And that was when the tears started. Hers. Not mine.

"Such claptrap. How very unkind of you, Clementine," she burst out through her stupidly attractive sobs.

It was ridiculous how good the woman looked while crying. I got all blotchy and red, but not the mystery gal in purple. She grew even more lovely. It wasn't fair. I still had no clue what the hell she was talking about, but on the off chance she might throw a tantrum if I asked more questions, I kept my mouth shut.

And yes, she had a point, but my *hygiene* was none of her damn business. I couldn't quite put my finger on the last time I'd showered. If I had to guess, it was probably in the last five to twelve days. I was on a deadline for a book. To be more precise, I was late for my deadline on a book. I didn't exactly have time for personal sanitation right now.

And speaking of deadlines...

"How about this?" My tone was excessively polite. I almost laughed. The woman had illegally entered my house, and I was behaving like she was a guest. "I'll take a shower later today after I get through a few pivotal chapters. Right now, you should leave so I can work."

"Yes, of course," she replied, absently stroking Fat Stella, who purred. If I'd done that, I would be minus a finger. "It would be dreadfully sad if you were under the hatches."

I nodded. "Right. That would, umm... suck."

The woman in purple smiled. It was radiant, and I would have sworn I heard birds happily chirping. I was losing it.

"Excellent," she said, pulling a small periwinkle velvet bag from her cleavage. I wondered what else she had stored in there and hoped there wasn't a weapon. "I shall leave you with two gold coins. While the Grape Nuts were tasty, I would prefer that you purchase some Lucky Charms. I understand they are magically delicious."

"It was you?" I asked, wildly relieved that I hadn't been sleep eating. I had enough problems at the moment. Gaining weight from midnight dates with cereal wasn't on the to-do list.

"It was," she confirmed, getting to her feet and dropping the coins into my hand. "The consistency was quite different from porridge, but I found it tasty—very crunchy."

"Right… well… thank you for putting the bowl in the sink." Wait. Why the hell was I thanking her? She'd wandered in and eaten my Grape Nuts.

"You are most welcome, Clementine," she said with a disarming smile that lit up her unusual eyes. "It was lovely finally meeting you even if your disheveled outward show is entirely astonishing."

I was reasonably sure I had just been insulted by the cereal lover, but it was presented with excellent manners. However, she did answer a question. We hadn't met. I wasn't sure why she seemed familiar. The fact that she knew my name was alarming.

"Are you a stalker?" I asked before I could stop myself.

I'd had a few over the years. Being a *New York Times* bestselling author was something I was proud of, but it had come with a little baggage here and there. Some people seemed to have difficulty discerning fiction from reality. If I had to guess, I'd say Purple Gal might be one of those people.

I'd only written one Regency novel, and that had been at the beginning of my career, before I'd found my groove in paranormal romance. I was way more comfortable writing about demons and vampires than people dressed in top hats and hoopskirts. Maybe the crazy woman had read my first book. It hadn't done well, and for good reason. It was over-the-top bad. I'd blocked the entire novel out of my mind. Live and learn. It had been my homage to Elizabeth Hoyt well over a decade ago. It had been clear to all that I should leave Regency romance to the masters.

"Don't be a Merry Andrew," the woman chided me. "Your bone box is addled. We must see to it at once. I shall pay a visit again soon."

The only part of her gibberish I understood was that she thought she was coming back. Note to self—change all the locks on the doors. Since it wasn't clear if she was packing heat in her cleavage, I just smiled and nodded.

"Alrighty then…" I was unsure if I should walk her to the door or if she would let herself out. Deciding it would be better to make sure she actually left instead of letting her hide in my pantry to finish off my cereal, I gestured to the door. "Follow me."

Thick Stella growled at me. I was so tempted to flip her off but thought it might earn another lecture from Purple Gal. It was more than enough to be lambasted for my appearance. I didn't need my manners picked apart by someone with a tenuous grip on reality.

My own grip was dubious as it was.

"You might want to reconsider breaking into homes," I said, holding the front door open. "It could end badly—for you."

Part of me couldn't believe that I was trying to help the

nutty woman out, but I couldn't seem to stop myself. I kind of liked her.

"I'll keep that in mind," she replied as she sauntered out of my house into the warm spring afternoon. "Remember, Clementine, there is always sunshine after the rain."

As she made her way down the long sunlit, tree-lined drive, she didn't look back. It was disturbingly like watching the end of a period movie where the heroine left her old life behind and walked proudly toward her new and promising future.

Glancing around for a car, I didn't spot one. Had she left it parked on the road so she could make a clean getaway after she'd bludgeoned me? Had I just politely escorted a murderer out of my house?

Had I lost it for real?

Probably.

As she disappeared from sight, I felt the weight of the gold coins still clutched in my hand. Today couldn't get any stranger.

At least, I hoped not.

Opening my fist to examine the coins, I gasped. "What in the heck?"

There was nothing in my hand.

Had I dropped them? Getting down on all fours, I searched. Thick Stella joined me, kind of—more like watched me as I crawled around and wondered if anything that had just happened had actually happened.

"Purple Gal gave me coins to buy Lucky Charms," I told my cat, my search now growing frantic. "You saw her do it. Right? She sat next to you. And you didn't attack her. *Right?*"

Thick Stella simply stared at me. What did I expect? If my cat answered me, I'd have to commit myself. That option might still be on the table. Had I just imagined the entire exchange with the strange woman? Should I call the cops?

"And tell them what?" I asked, standing back up and locking the front door securely. "That a woman in a purple gown broke in and ate my cereal while politely insulting my hygiene? Oh, and she left me two gold coins that disappeared in my hand as soon as she was out of sight? That's not going to work."

I'd call the police if she came back, since I wasn't sure she'd been here at all. She hadn't threatened to harm me. Purple Gal had been charming and well-mannered the entire time she'd badmouthed my cleanliness habits. And to be quite honest, real or not, she'd made a solid point. I could use a shower.

Maybe four months of wallowing in self-pity and only living inside the fictional worlds I created on paper had taken more of a toll than I was aware of. Getting lost in my stories was one of my favorite things to do. It had saved me more than once over the years. It was possible that I'd let it go too far. Hence, the Purple Gal hallucination.

Shit.

First things first. Delete Candy Jelly Crush. Getting rid of the white noise in my life was the first step to… well, the first step to something.

I'd figure it out later.

HIT HERE TO ORDER THE WRITE HOOK!!!!!

ROBYN'S BOOK LIST

(IN CORRECT READING ORDER)

HOT DAMNED SERIES
Fashionably Dead
Fashionably Dead Down Under
Hell on Heels
Fashionably Dead in Diapers
A Fashionably Dead Christmas
Fashionably Hotter Than Hell
Fashionably Dead and Wed
Fashionably Fanged
Fashionably Flawed
A Fashionably Dead Diary
Fashionably Forever After
Fashionably Fabulous
A Fashionable Fiasco
Fashionably Fooled
Fashionably Dead and Loving It
Fashionably Dead and Demonic

The Oh My Gawd Couple
A Fashionable Disaster

GOOD TO THE LAST DEMON SERIES
As the Underworld Turns
The Edge of Evil
The Bold and the Banished
Guiding Blight

GOOD TO THE LAST DEATH SERIES
It's a Wonderful Midlife Crisis
Whose Midlife Crisis Is It Anyway?
A Most Excellent Midlife Crisis
My Midlife Crisis, My Rules
You Light Up My Midlife Crisis
It's A Matter of Midlife and Death
The Facts Of Midlife
It's A Hard Knock Midlife
Run for Your Midlife
It's A Hell of A Midlife

MY SO-CALLED MYSTICAL MIDLIFE SERIES
The Write Hook
You May Be Write
All The Write Moves
My Big Fat Hairy Wedding

SHIFT HAPPENS SERIES
Ready to Were
Some Were in Time

No Were To Run
Were Me Out
Were We Belong

MAGIC AND MAYHEM SERIES

Switching Hour
Witch Glitch
A Witch in Time
Magically Delicious
A Tale of Two Witches
Three's A Charm
Switching Witches
You're Broom or Mine?
The Bad Boys of Assjacket
The Newly Witch Game
Witches In Stitches

SEA SHENANIGANS SERIES

Tallulah's Temptation
Ariel's Antics
Misty's Mayhem
Petunia's Pandemonium
Jingle Me Balls

A WYLDE PARANORMAL SERIES

Beauty Loves the Beast

HANDCUFFS AND HAPPILY EVER AFTERS SERIES

How Hard Can it Be?
Size Matters

Cop a Feel

If after reading all the above you are still wanting more adventure and zany fun, read *Pirate Dave and His Randy Adventures*, the romance novel budding novelist Rena helped wicked Evangeline write in *How Hard Can It Be?*

Warning: Pirate Dave Contains Romance Satire, Spoofing, and Pirates with Two Pork Swords.

NOTE FROM THE AUTHOR

If you enjoyed reading *Guiding Blight*, please consider leaving a positive review or rating on the site where you purchased it. Reader reviews help my books continue to be valued by resellers and help new readers make decisions about reading them.

You are the reason I write these stories and I sincerely appreciate each of you!

Many thanks for your support,
~ Robyn Peterman

Want to hear about my new releases?
Visit https://robynpeterman.com/newsletter/ and join my mailing list!

ABOUT ROBYN PETERMAN

Robyn Peterman writes because the people inside her head won't leave her alone until she gives them life on paper. Her addictions include laughing really hard with friends, shoes (the expensive kind), Target, Coke (the drink not the drug LOL) with extra ice in a Yeti cup, bejeweled reading glasses, her kids, her super-hot hubby and collecting stray animals.

A former professional actress with Broadway, film and T.V. credits, she now lives in the South with her family and too many animals to count.

Writing gives her peace and makes her whole, plus having a job where she can work in sweatpants is perfect for her.

Made in the USA
Las Vegas, NV
09 January 2024